SILENCED WITNESS

Morven Jennings is a super recogniser: she has the ability to remember the faces of almost everyone she's ever seen. Having lived under an assumed identity in witness protection since the murder of her parents when she was sixteen, she hopes one day to spot the face of the killer in a CCTV image. But when her investigation of the abduction of a baby from Heathrow Airport takes her down unexpected avenues, it brings shadows of her past to light — and puts her in the sights of dangerous enemies . . .

Books by Tracey Walsh
in the Linford Romance Library:

TROUBLE IN PARADISE

TRACEY WALSH

SILENCED WITNESS

Complete and Unabridged

LINFORD
Leicester

First published in Great Britain in 2017

First Linford Edition
published 2020

A catalogue record for this book is available from the British Library.

ISBN 978–1–4448–4460–3

Published by
Ulverscroft Limited
Anstey, Leicestershire

Set by Words & Graphics Ltd.
Anstey, Leicestershire
Printed and bound in Great Britain by
T. J. International Ltd., Padstow, Cornwall

This book is printed on acid-free paper

1

Carly was awake before her alarm this morning even though it was set to some ridiculous hour. She couldn't wait to leave the house and her shift started very early, so she was gone long before her mum and dad were up.

Immaculate in her ground crew uniform, sitting proudly at the check-in desk, she still can't quite believe she's a part of all this.

Beyond the Passport Control barriers, deeper into the terminal, dozens of security staff perform the rigorous procedures designed to prevent terrorist attacks on a flight.

Meanwhile back in check-in, a handful of officers observe the thousands of people arriving at the terminal buildings.

Flashing her best welcoming smile at the next passenger as he lifts his bags onto the conveyor belt, Carly switches her attention for a second towards the entrance to the terminal. It appears that there's some sort of argument going on between two men.

Carly hopes they'll join someone else's queue and concentrates on the task in hand.

Five seconds later, she barely has the time to wonder why she's no longer at her desk before everything fades to black.

2

As the smoke cleared there was an instant of complete silence before all hell broke loose.

Alarms wailed, triggered by what everyone instantly thought was a bomb but was actually a high impact 'flash bang' device, designed to create the maximum noise, smoke and a blinding light.

Its purpose was to create a diversion. The police and security forces use them when they break up a siege or crowd trouble.

Morven Jennings had the benefit of hindsight so she knew she wasn't looking at the aftermath of an explosion. Seated at her desk in the super recognisers' team office she viewed the CCTV images again.

She lost count long ago of how many times she'd run the digital file containing the images from Heathrow Airport

Terminal Two that morning.

At 07:35 three men entered the terminal building. One immediately turned on his heel and left. The other two walked towards the check-in desks engaged in a heated conversation.

When they reached the queues they seemed to search for a particular person before moving in and setting off the flash bang. There was only one casualty and the two men couldn't have predicted what would happen.

As the device went off, the young woman behind the check-in desk rolled backwards on her chair at high speed and hit the wall behind her. The head injury caused by the impact was fatal.

As people started to recover from the shock they became aware of a woman screaming. But she wasn't injured. She was shouting over and over again, 'My baby! They've taken my baby!'

Morven had already taken in everything about the CCTV images. Her next task was to look through the Persons of Interest files, hoping to find a match to the three subjects she was studying on the CCTV.

Super recognisers have a rare talent — the ability to remember the faces of almost everyone they have ever seen. The Metropolitan Police employs a task force of these people, who can recall up to ninety-five per cent of the faces they've seen compared to just twenty per cent for the average person.

Hours later, after poring over images until her eyes were burning, Morven had to admit that the three she was searching for were not in the files. Typing her report into the investigation team's database, Morven felt the usual frustration building. When she couldn't find a match, she took it personally. Every single time.

The supervisor approached her desk with a long-suffering look on her face.

'Come on, Morven,' Sergeant Foster said. 'Shift ended half an hour ago. Don't you have a home to go to?' Same comment every day.

'Okay, Sarge. I'm off now,' Morven

said as she gathered her things together and reluctantly headed for the door.

As she walked to the lifts she couldn't stop herself glancing into Detective Inspector Bradley's office. The lights were off and the place was deserted. Unusual for him to leave so early, she thought, then made a conscious effort to tear her eyes away and carry on out of the building.

Morven's schoolgirl crush on the senior officer in her team was becoming annoying even to herself. She only hoped that none of her colleagues had picked up on it.

Dave Bradley had interviewed Morven when she applied to join the team and for months she had treated him the same as any other senior officer.

Then suddenly she had found herself noticing when he wasn't there, or looking forward to coming in to work early on a Monday morning. DI Bradley was always the first one in and Morven would try to engineer it so that she wasn't far behind him. On a really good day, she would manage to grab a coffee and a chat with him before anyone else arrived.

There were a few problems with this situation — chiefly that he was her boss, so there was no chance of starting a relationship. Even if he had been interested in her.

* * *

Waiting at the local Chinese restaurant to pick up the order she'd phoned in on the way, Morven glanced idly at the TV screen above the counter. It was tuned to a twenty-four-hour news channel showing an interview with some politician or other.

Morven had seen his face before — today. On the Heathrow CCTV film. He was 'the third man', the one who left immediately while the other two entered the terminal. It didn't make any sense but Morven was certain.

She took out her phone and snapped a photo of the TV screen showing the man's face clearly. Then she thanked

Mr Hon and left.

Minutes later, Morven pressed the entry code buttons to open the gate into the forecourt of the apartment block. If any of her colleagues saw where she lived they'd be amazed. The penthouse apartment with river views from the balcony was way beyond the means of a police constable.

If asked, she'd explain it away by saying she was house-sitting for a wealthy relative, but that would be a lie. No, she lived here courtesy of her inheritance from her parents who died when she was just sixteen years old.

Ten years on, the pain had hardly diminished — for Morven had witnessed the cold-blooded murder of both her parents.

Of course, she wasn't Morven then. That was in another lifetime. The image of her parents' killer was burned into her brain, but no matter how many mug shots the police showed her, he had never been caught.

Courtesy of the Protected Persons

Service, or witness protection scheme as it was more commonly known, Elly Clarke had been reborn as Morven Jennings. Her liaison officer had discovered her remarkable super-recogniser talents during counselling and assessment sessions over the next couple of years, and had steered her in the direction of her current role.

Although, financially, she had no need to work, it hadn't taken Morven long to realise it was the perfect job for her. With access to literally millions of CCTV and still images gathered by police forces around the country, she was sure that one day she would find him. The man who killed her parents and stole her life.

Until that day she would put her talents to good use, helping to put away those who had wrecked other people's lives . . .

3

Next morning Morven got up early. As she jogged beside the river, she felt the benefit of the exercise on both her mind and body.

Perhaps if she ran for long enough, it would clear her mind of the recurring dreams about Dave Bradley that had disturbed her all night.

She was unable to control what she dreamed about, of course, but these dreams were so vivid and romantic that she sometimes found herself blushing when she recalled them the next day.

It was a new experience for Morven to be so enthralled by a man. She'd had a few boyfriends back when she was Elly, but nothing serious. In fact, they were really just friends who happened to be boys. The years since then, with hardly a hint of romance or flirtation, made her current unrequited feelings all the harder to cope with.

She'd had a few flings with men her work colleagues had set her up with on blind dates — enough to mean she wasn't completely clueless when it came to romance — but as far as being in love was concerned, she was a complete novice.

Her running route finished with a gentle climb back up from the river and gave her a great view. Not for the first time, Morven acknowledged how grateful she was to be able to live in such a pleasant neighbourhood.

A little voice at the back of her mind reminded her that she could only afford it because of her parents' deaths. It was always the same. Any happiness she felt was tempered by a constant guilt that she was still here while they had gone.

When she was being rational, she knew that her mum and dad would have wanted her to survive, but sometimes it was hard to remember.

Returning home and showering quickly, she prepared breakfast and settled down to eat while catching up with the TV news. The same politician from the night before was now on the local news.

The abduction of the baby at Heathrow had apparently been made public, though Morven was sure the boss would have wanted a news blackout at this stage. The guy's name popped up on a caption on the screen — John Whitehouse, MP for the borough where Morven lived.

She felt guilty for a moment at her lack of knowledge. Surely she should know her own MP? But that thought was chased away by more important questions. Why was someone who she was sure had been at Heathrow yesterday giving interviews about the abduction today?

All thoughts of breakfast were dropped as Morven reached for her work phone. She was supposed to be off-duty until Monday but this was too important to wait. She got through to the incident room and explained what she had just seen to one of the detectives, offering to come in if necessary.

* * *

Morven arrived at the incident room halfway through the team briefing and took a seat at the back of the room, hoping to speak to the DI when he'd finished. However DI Bradley had been briefed about Morven's identification of one of the airport subjects and beckoned her forward.

Muttering a silent curse, she joined him at the front of the room — she hated being centre of attention and having to speak to a large group of people. And there was always the fear that someone might notice how she reacted when she was near Dave Bradley.

Clearing her throat, she gave it her best shot.

'John Whitehouse MP is, in my opinion, the same man who was seen just inside Heathrow Terminal Two seconds before the two others set off the device and abducted the child.' She turned to attach to a display board a photograph she had printed on her way to the incident room.

There were murmurs of disbelief.

'That airport CCTV image of him just shows his profile as he turns away. How can you be so sure?' Bradley asked.

'I'm not going to bore you with the stats about how accurate my team's identifications are. But believe me, we've positively ID'd suspects on far less than that. My colleagues and I can make a match based on an image showing just an ear or an eyebrow . . .' Morven realised she was sounding defensive so she stopped mid-sentence.

Bradley took over again.

'Thanks, PC Jennings. You've given us a lot to think about. Now all we have to do is work out a) why a respected politician would be involved in an abduction, b) who his accomplices are — and c) where the hell the child is.'

There were a few snorts of laughter, rapidly disguised as coughs. Morven blushed a deep red and made a hasty exit from the room.

* * *

Sitting at her desk reliving the last few minutes in her head, Morven feared that she'd just set back the reputation of the super recogniser team beyond repair. Sergeant Foster would have her guts for garters come Monday. Why hadn't she followed the correct procedure? What she should have done was update the database and alert her supervisor to the possible ID she'd made.

Instead she'd gone directly to the boss of the investigating team, convinced she was a hundred per cent correct in her identification. Always quick to analyse her own actions, Morven feared she had been trying to impress Dave Bradley rather than acting in the best interests of her team.

Morven sat with her head in her hands for a few minutes before resigning herself to a dressing down on Monday.

* * *

John Whitehouse was reflecting on a roller-coaster couple of days. On the plus side, the abduction plan had succeeded beautifully. He had just leaked to the press what had happened, claiming to have the information from an anonymous source. He knew the police would want to keep all information under their control until the kidnappers made contact.

However he also knew that the men who had abducted the child would not be contacting anyone. It was vitally important to John Whitehouse that the kidnapping should be publicised as widely as possible. He was absolutely certain that his alibi for the time of the abduction would stand up to scrutiny. Now all he had to do was wait for the others to play their part.

* * *

Morven let herself into the apartment and set down her shopping bags on the kitchen island. As usual, a little retail therapy had cheered her up and put her work problems into proportion. She'd been quite restrained today — a shopping spree usually involved spending much more.

Her flatmate, Paula, had dragged herself out of bed. She busied herself making coffee while pretending not to stare.

'You OK, Morven?' she asked solicitously.

Morven was thrown for a second by her serious tone. Paula was usually happy-go-lucky; there wasn't much that could darken her mood.

Paula continued, 'I saw the news. The fire.' She put an arm around Morven's shoulder.

After a few more seconds of confusion, Morven spotted the local paper on the table and realised where Paula was coming from. The headline screamed about a serious house fire nearby.

She'd never told Paula the truth about her family history. Instead she'd told her the same cover story she always told everyone — that her parents were killed in a house fire. It explained why she had no photos or mementoes and stopped people questioning further.

For a moment she felt a pang of guilt at misleading Paula. Then she reminded herself that protecting her identity was potentially a matter of life or death. It was only by sticking to her cover absolutely all the time that she was able to have any peace of mind at all.

'It's OK,' she said. 'I can't let every family's tragedy drag me back to mine.'

Nevertheless, now that Paula had compared last night's house fire to her own situation, Morven couldn't help her mood being dragged down again. She was still embarrassed about making an idiot of herself at work, but she couldn't discuss this with Paula. It would be unprofessional, and how could she expect Paula to understand why she was so driven in her attitude to searching CCTV images when she hadn't even told her the real reason why she was obsessed by the work?

All these thoughts spun around Morven's head as she stood with Paula's protective arm around her. Not for the first time, she was thankful that her witness protection liaison officer had suggested finding a flatmate. Morven had been struggling for a while and feeling lonely. Her usual liaison officer, Jenny, had gone on maternity leave and her replacement, Ben, had suggested the new living arrangement at one of their early meetings.

'I think it would do you good to have company,' Ben had said. 'And it's great timing because my cousin, Paula, is looking for a place.'

It seemed fate was telling her it was a good idea. That had been two months ago and the two women were now friends. But had she known the thoughts occupying Paula's head at that moment, Morven would have realised that she had far more to worry about than a bad day at work.

4

The rest of the weekend passed in a flurry of domestic activity and TV box set binges.

Morven could have employed a cleaner, of course, but she preferred to do her own housework and her standards verged on OCD. Paula was the opposite, so Morven refused to set foot in her room or the en-suite bathroom.

Saturday evening found the two women slumped on matching sofas in front of the TV, arguing half-heartedly over whose turn it was to venture into the kitchen in search of snacks. They'd slipped into a comfortable friendship so easily. Morven thought how grateful she was to Ben for suggesting the arrangement.

Paula was very happy, of course. She was living in a luxury flat for the level of rent she would have paid in a grotty student house-share. And Morven was happy because she no longer had to endure that sinking feeling that used to come every time she let herself into an empty home.

Comfortable in the glow of the wine and a delicious meal, Morven looked around the sitting room with a contented sigh. She loved the fact that it was a brand new apartment when she'd bought it and nobody else had put the stamp of their personality on it.

When she moved in, the place was basically an empty shell. The developers had wanted to decorate and furnish it as a show flat but when Morven turned up and paid cash for it, they were happy to switch their plans to the floor below.

She had spent many happy hours browsing websites and stores until she came up with exactly the right item she wanted for every inch of the place. She couldn't understand why people paid interior designers to do it all for them — it was fun!

Her favourite things of all in the

room were the pair of deep, squashy sofas. They had been made to order, which meant she had sat on a deckchair for the first few weeks. But now her greatest luxury when she arrived home from a hard day at work was to sink into one of the cream and brown seats, kick off her shoes and lie back for a few minutes.

If there was one slight irritation with having Paula there, it was that Morven hardly ever had the apartment to herself any more. Paula was meant to be studying at a college a few miles away, but her timetable seemed to be very generous on free time.

Most of the time, the two women made their own meals. It was too much hassle to try and make their meal times coincide with Morven's late evenings at the office. However at weekends, they made the effort and took it in turns to cook something special.

Morven sometimes wondered about Paula's lack of a social life. As a student, shouldn't her weekends be one long list of parties and hangovers? But Ben had hinted at Paula's confidence having taken a battering from a bad relationship, and Morven hadn't wanted to bring up the subject.

That night's feast had been created by Paula who had somehow managed to do a huge food shop in less than half an hour. She was one of those people who would always find the quickest way to do everything. If only she would apply that to cleaning her room occasionally, Morven thought she would be the perfect flatmate.

Now they were rounding off the evening with a few glasses of wine and conversation turned to affairs of the heart.

Although they'd only known each other a short time, Morven felt she could easily start to see Paula as the kid sister she'd never had. It would be nice to have a bond like that with someone. It was hard to explain, though she suspected that it was partly due to the fact that she'd never let anyone close for such a long time.

Since her parents' deaths and her enforced new identity, Morven hadn't felt able to trust anyone enough to become friends. With Paula it was different. As soon as she had turned up at the apartment that first day, weighed down by bags, the two had got on like a house on fire. Their weekly girls' nights in had cemented the friendship. It was time for Morven to let down her defences.

'Paula, there's a guy at work who's driving me crazy. I don't know what to do,' she said, avoiding eye contact by pouring more wine.

'DI Bradley, by any chance?' Paula asked.

'How did — '

'You can barely have a conversation without dropping his name in,' Paula said. 'You don't even know you're doing it.'

Morven was mortified. Paula was right — she hadn't noticed that she'd being talking about the DI at home.

What if she'd been doing the same at work? The others were probably laughing at her behind her back and gossiping.

Oh no — what if Dave Bradley himself was aware of it?

'Relax,' Paula said. 'You're far too professional and, well, secretive to talk about that stuff at work. I mean, it's only been the past couple of weeks that I've started to notice your obsession with him.'

'It's not an obsession,' Morven objected. Then she noticed the grin on Paula's face and realised she was winding her up. She whacked Paula round the head with a cushion and they both dissolved into laughter.

'For what it's worth,' Paula said when they'd recovered, 'I don't think it's ever a good idea to have a relationship with someone you work with. It never ends well.' A shadow passed over Paula's face and despite all the wine they'd drunk, she seemed to have sobered up all of a sudden.

'You sound so worldly-wise,' Morven said. 'But you're even younger than me. Do you want to tell me what happened to make you so cynical about romance?'

Paula sighed, then seemed to decide that the conversation had become far too serious.

'Some other time maybe,' she said. 'Now I'm off to bed. Your turn to clear up in the kitchen, right?'

Morven groaned. Paula was a fabulous cook but she had a habit of using every single utensil in the drawers and cupboards. The deal was that whoever cooked, the other cleaned up.

Tonight Morven couldn't face it. She'd get up early and deal with it in the morning. She decided this was a good sign — maybe her OCD was showing signs of improvement.

As she drifted off to sleep, Morven realised that something Paula had said didn't make sense. Paula had said that having a relationship with someone you work with never ends well. Yet she was a student, and as far as Morven knew she'd never had a job in her life — not even a part time one to offset her student loan.

Odd, Morven thought as she finally

gave in to sleep. By the time she woke up next morning she'd forgotten it completely.

* * *

Paula was out all day Sunday, which was such an unusual occurrence that Morven was determined to make the most of it by lounging around in her own space without anyone to disturb her.

Once she'd dealt with the chaos in the kitchen she tried to spend the leisurely day she had promised herself, but after a couple of hours she became restless. She was trying not to think about the telling-off she was due to get the next day at work so she needed to find something to do to take her mind off it.

As usual, she turned to cleaning and tidying as a way of distracting herself. The apartment was already pristine but that didn't stop her spending hours making sure it stayed that way.

She was in bed by the time she heard Paula come in. This was the great thing about having a flatmate, she thought, feeling more positive again. It was comforting to know there was someone else around, yet they didn't have to live in each other's pockets. However, she didn't entirely trust Paula to lock up properly so she slipped out of bed and went to check the front door.

On her way back, as she passed Paula's bedroom door, she heard hushed voices. She'd never talked to Paula about bringing boyfriends home. She realised now that, although she wasn't too happy about it, any twenty-something person would expect to be able to bring friends or partners home.

Morven felt like an over-protective parent — or, more likely, she envied the fact that Paula was in a relationship. Whatever — she needed to deal with her feelings about it, and quickly.

She didn't want to jeopardise her friendship with Paula. She resolved to be tolerant, but a small voice in her head whispered that it might have been nice if Paula had asked if it was OK to bring someone back before doing it.

Perhaps the novelty of having a flatmate was starting to wear off after all. But how could Morven change her mind about having Paula living here? She wouldn't just be letting Paula down by making her homeless. Ben had thought he was helping by suggesting the arrangement, so she'd be upsetting him too.

Morven's problem was that she was sometimes too nice for her own good. She knew she'd probably just let things carry on as they were so she didn't risk hurting anyone's feelings.

* * *

Monday morning's alarm dragged Morven from a dream where she was opening all the doors in the apartment and behind each one was a different, faceless man. She didn't need a psychologist to interpret that for her.

She was up and out of the apartment

in record time, determined to be at work before anyone else. However as she entered the team's office it was already a hive of activity.

The child who'd been abducted was still missing. Most of the detectives on the case had worked all weekend and were in early for the start of a new week. The super recogniser section of the team, to which Morven belonged, were the only ones able to work fairly normal office hours.

DI Bradley had noticed her arrival and he headed over to her desk a few minutes later.

'PC Jennings,' he said. 'A word, please.' He walked towards his office at the corner of the large room and Morven followed, her mouth going dry as she anticipated the next few minutes.

'Office' was a bit of an overstatement. The DI's work area was more of a goldfish bowl divided from the rest of the team by two glass walls. Several pairs of eyes followed the two of them as they headed towards it.

'Take a seat, Morven,' Dave Bradley said. He hardly ever used her first name — *good or bad*? she wondered. 'I wanted to apologise for the other day,' he continued and Morven's eyes widened in surprise. 'We're all stressed by the case and I used that as an excuse to show you up in front of the team. No, let me finish,' he said as Morven tried to interrupt. 'You were doing your job and you gave up part of a rest day to come in. You deserve credit for that. But — and it's a big but — you can't go around accusing members of parliament of kidnapping babies without a lot more evidence than a two-second CCTV clip. OK?'

A dozen possible replies sprang to Morven's mind but she knew Dave well enough to choose the only one he'd accept. 'OK.'

'Great. I want you at the briefing at eight. There's a press conference at nine-thirty and then we'll take it from there.'

Morven knew this was her cue to go

back to her own desk.

'Coffee?' she asked, cringing inside as she realised she was trying to prolong their one-to-one conversation.

'Just had one, thanks.'

He was already absorbed in a message that had appeared on his laptop screen.

Morven took a last glance at Dave's tousled hair and crumpled shirt as she left his office. He'd obviously been there all night. Yet she knew he kept several changes of clothes here and if there was going to be a press conference, he'd be showered and changed by the time it started and looking fresh as a daisy.

* * *

John Whitehouse MP switched on the TV in his office at Westminster. The police were due to give a press conference that morning. He wanted to make sure things were progressing as he'd expected. He'd been disappointed at the lack of news coverage over the weekend.

Surely the abduction of a baby from one of the world's busiest airports was worthy of more attention? The tragic death of a check-in worker had barely rated a mention either.

Whitehouse sighed. That had never been part of the plan and it had potentially changed everything. Nobody could have predicted that someone would suffer a fatal head injury. Nobody was supposed to have got hurt.

He'd leave the TV on so he didn't miss the start of the press conference. This channel usually showed an empty table in front of the Met Police's logo banner for ages before these things. He glanced at his watch, then reached into his pocket for his mobile phone.

His second mobile phone, that is — the one that couldn't be traced to him, and that had just one contact number saved on it.

Just a quick call, he told himself. He'd feel better once he knew that their young guest was doing OK.

5

The early morning briefing was the chance for the Senior Investigating Officer to bring the whole team up to date with the investigation. It was also an opportunity for everyone to put forward their ideas for how to take things forward.

But ultimately the buck stopped with DI Bradley and it was up to him to keep the top brass up to speed. After the briefing Dave would have ten minutes to feed back progress, or lack of it, to his boss before heading to the press conference. It was a stressful, high-pressure role but he thrived on it.

He'd been asked to think about going for promotion more than once, even though he'd already risen through the ranks incredibly quickly, but he knew he'd miss having his finger on the pulse of every ongoing investigation.

He glanced up and through the glass wall of his office and was proud to see that virtually the whole team was already sitting waiting for the briefing to start. They were the best bunch of people he'd had the pleasure to work with and over the past couple of years, he'd moulded them into an effective team.

They weren't perfect, of course, but they all came to work determined to give a hundred percent. He'd weeded out a couple of bad 'uns on the way. Only last month there had been that unpleasant situation that had led to one detective constable being transferred back to uniform and another being kicked off the force completely. He didn't want to go through that again in a hurry.

Yet the successes more than made up for the failures. His decision to take on a small team of super recognisers, for instance. Sergeant Foster and her team of three were now an important part of his department.

Dave rubbed his eyes as he tried not to get distracted by the one potential problem with the super recogniser team. PC Morven Jennings. As good as, if not better than her colleagues at the job, Morven was hopefully unaware of the difficulty she was causing him.

He'd been attracted to her from the first moment she walked into the interview room a year or so ago. The interviews were just a formality so he hadn't needed to worry that he'd shown any bias. But he'd given himself a good talking to over the next couple of weeks before the super recognisers moved into the team's office.

There were bound to be situations where colleagues became attracted to each other. Dave's own parents had met at work like countless other couples. However he took his responsibilities as a people manager very seriously. He was in a position of influence over those he managed, and it would be unprofessional to allow emotions to encroach on the workplace.

He nearly managed to convince himself. Hopefully no-one else was aware of the struggle he faced each working day.

Shaking these thoughts from his head, Dave shrugged on his suit jacket and walked through to the main office. The buzz of conversation died down and everyone's attention was fixed on him within seconds.

'Good morning, all. It's eight a.m. on Monday the sixth of March and this is the second full briefing of Operation Bellevue.'

Code names for major investigations were randomly allocated by a computer programme, the name usually only being rejected if it had some inappropriate connotation or a connection to the victims.

'I'll be allocating actions shortly,' DI Bradley continued. 'But first, a quick summary to make sure we're all singing from the same hymn sheet. Last Friday morning, one-year-old Ayesha Khalil was abducted from Heathrow Airport. A flash bang device was used as a diversion and this led to the death of Carly Simmonds, a twenty-year-old check-in worker.'

Nods around the room showed that everyone was keeping up.

'Ayesha and her mother were returning home to Dubai after spending the past two weeks at their family's London base, a flat in Kensington.' He consulted his notes. 'Windsor Towers.'

Morven's eyes flew up from the notepad she'd been scribbling notes in. Windsor Towers was the next block to her apartment. Still, it was just a coincidence and she didn't want to draw attention to where she lived, so she kept quiet.

Then another thought struck her. Was that why her local MP was so interested in the case? If the victims had a residence in his constituency it would explain his involvement. Yet she had linked John Whitehouse to the case before she was aware of his interest.

Confused, she focused her attention back on what Dave Bradley was saying.

'Ayesha's mother, Yasmeen Khalil,

will be here shortly to take part in the press conference. I've had Rachel Roberts with her as liaison officer most of the weekend, as she's obviously in a fragile state. I'm not convinced it'll do any good having her on the panel but I'm under orders from the media team to have her there.'

'Does she speak English?' someone piped up from the back of the room.

'Better than you or me, I expect,' Dave said with a wry grin. 'She was educated in England — boarding school up north. Funnily enough it was that school where those murders took place last Christmas.'

'No connection there, boss, I've been chasing up that angle all weekend but there's nothing. Straight after leaving school she went back home. Marriage to the son of family friends had been on the cards since they were both toddlers.'

'Where is the dad?' came another question from one of the team, all of whom were intent on piecing all the bits of information together.

'He stayed behind in Dubai. He runs a racing stable. Has several billionaire clients including his uncle who also happens to be minor royalty. The dad, er, Hamid Khalil, is on his way over — due to land any time now.'

For the second time Morven's attention was grabbed by a particular detail of what was being said. She'd spent the hour before the briefing researching everything she could find about John Whitehouse, working back from his election to parliament two years ago to his family background.

She'd learned that he grew up living at his father's training stables in Newmarket. After his father died at the relatively young age of sixty, the brother, Mark Whitehouse, had taken over the stables and was now one of the most successful trainers in the country.

Could horse racing be a connection between the Khalil family and the MP? Morven weighed up the pros and cons and decided it was too important to ignore.

'Boss,' she said, blushing as usual when everyone's attention turned to her. She cleared her throat. 'John Whitehouse has strong family links to the racehorse training community. Added to the CCTV from Heathrow, isn't that enough for us to look at him?'

Dave Bradley rolled his eyes.

'We talked about this earlier, PC Jennings. I thought I made myself clear. Tens of thousands of people have links to the horse racing business. Instead of turning up tenuous links to the MP, you need something to keep you busy. Sit in on the press conference. I have a job for you straight afterwards. Now, to sum up,' he continued, addressing the whole team, 'we currently have zero leads and zero suspects. I think our most sensible line of enquiry is to assume the kidnappers targeted the Khalil family because of their mega-rich uncle. I'm just surprised there's been no ransom demand as yet.

'I'm late for my update meeting with She Who Must Be Obeyed upstairs.

Check this list for your actions and let's get on with it.'

He stuck an A4 sheet of paper to the virtually blank display board behind him and left the room.

While everyone milled about preparing to get on with their allocated tasks, Morven slumped in her chair trying to get her head around her feelings for Dave Bradley. It was starting to affect her ability to do her job properly. Maybe she should speak to Sergeant Foster about moving back to the main super recogniser team.

Yet that would mean going back to sitting in front of her computer screen all day, every day. And while her main motivation for doing the job was the opportunity to access CCTV from police forces all over the country, she had to admit that she'd been more fulfilled this past year. She was part of the major crimes team and although her main role was still the CCTV work, she'd been able to contribute to investigations in other ways.

However she didn't know how much longer she would be able to cope with the way Dave Bradley ridiculed her in front of the rest of the team, despite his apology earlier. She never saw him treat anyone else that way. And what did it say about Morven and her self-esteem that she was willing to endure it? It was a question that had kept her awake at night, but she had yet to come up with an answer that didn't depress her.

She could hardly believe it had been a year since her move to this team. She glanced around the office, remembering the first time she had walked in — the new kid desperate to make a good impression.

Well, she still felt that way a lot of the time but at least she had settled into her surroundings. The office was huge, taking up the whole of one floor of the police station. It was mostly open plan apart from a few small meeting areas and of course Dave Bradley's glass compartment.

Morven used to love watching TV

crime dramas but she'd had to give them up because she spent most of the time shouting at the screen, 'It's not like that,' or 'They wouldn't do that.'

On TV, a murder or major crime investigation team was always a cosy set-up of about ten people. In reality there were dozens sharing this space. Maybe they had to save money on how many actors they employed, she thought.

Another thing they always got wrong was family photos displayed on desks. Hardly any of her colleagues brought in photos — it was as if they were trying to protect their loved ones from coming into contact with the harrowing details of some of the crimes they investigated.

As far as décor went, the major crimes office was pretty bland and anonymous, with hard-wearing dark grey carpets and pale blue painted walls. Being a modern building most of the walls were taken up with huge, double glazed windows with white vertical blinds.

There was an interactive white board in the meeting area but it was hardly ever used; the boss preferred to stick to the old-fashioned method of sticking photos and other information to the display boards. Morven suspected he couldn't use the white board but he refused to admit it.

So it was nothing special, but this office housed some of the best and hardest-working officers in the Met. And Morven was a part of it. It would be a shame to say goodbye to that just because she couldn't keep her emotions in check.

She thought back to an evening a few months earlier. Until then, although she'd acknowledged that she was attracted to Dave, she'd been able to keep any inappropriate thoughts under control. But then came the night when the whole team were out celebrating the successful end to a case they'd been working on for months.

It was the usual pattern for the major crimes team. During a case it was noses to the grindstone, working every hour God sent. But an important part of the teamwork came later and it wasn't so much rewarding themselves for a job well done, but more an acknowledgement that everyone had played their part.

Cases could drag on for a long time and this one had been particularly gruelling. Everyone was letting their hair down and having a few too many drinks. At one point she ended up deep in conversation with Dave Bradley and she knew, somehow, that all she had to do was give him the right signal and they could have left the bar together.

And then who knew what might have happened? It was one of the few chances Morven had had to get to know Dave better and she certainly liked what she was getting to know. She'd gone to the Ladies' to splash her face with cold water and try to think calmly about the situation. When she made her way back, having decided to go for it, she was just in time to see Dave leave with a woman she'd never seen before.

Eyes stinging with disappointment and

humiliation, Morven waited five minutes to make sure Dave and his girlfriend had gone and then went outside to find a taxi.

Since then she had seen the mystery woman pick Dave up from work a couple of times and she'd given herself a stern talking-to. The reality check had come just in time to save her from making a stupid mistake.

Frustratingly, her heart continued to ignore her head and her feelings for the boss were as strong as ever.

It was nearly time for the press conference to start so Morven made her way to the media room and found a seat near the door. Whatever task DI Bradley had planned for her, she was determined to do it well and get back into his good books.

Waiting to one side of the room was the liaison officer, Rachel Roberts, talking quietly to a beautiful dark-haired woman who was hugging her coat around herself. Morven recognised Yasmeen Khalil from the Heathrow

CCTV footage. Unsurprisingly, she looked as if she hadn't slept since the abduction of her baby daughter.

The rest of the room was filled with reporters, some holding microphones, and several TV cameras aimed towards the table at the front.

The conference should have started by now. Morven assumed that the DI had been delayed by his boss demanding to know why no progress had been made in the investigation. Finally he arrived and ushered Yasmeen towards the table, ensuring she was comfortable before sitting down himself.

Rachel Roberts took the third chair and busied herself pouring glasses of water for the three of them. She was shattered after spending the whole weekend with Yasmeen Khalil, but the DI had promised her a break for the rest of the day. Her involvement in the press conference was simply to be on hand in case Yasmeen lost it in the face of the flashing cameras and the onslaught of questions.

‘Good morning, I’m Detective Inspector Dave Bradley of the Metropolitan Police major crimes team,’ Dave began. He’d organised enough of these events to be completely calm and assured. ‘As you all know, last Friday one-year-old Ayesha Khalil was abducted from the check-in area at Heathrow Airport Terminal Three. We have made available a short CCTV film that shows the people we are looking for in connection with this.’

Dave glanced to his left to make sure Yasmeen was up to facing the next part of the conference. She gave a barely discernible nod.

‘I’d now like to hand over to Ayesha’s mother, Yasmeen, who would like to say a few words.’

‘To the people who have my baby,’ Yasmeen said, reading from notes she had scribbled down earlier. ‘Please let the police know she is safe and well. I beg you to give her back to me. She is my life.’ Her voice broke on these last words and the tears began to fall.

Rachel Roberts put an arm around her and Dave Bradley took over again.

'If you have any questions I can give you five minutes now, and we will have a press release for you later this morning.'

From her place at the back of the room, Morven looked on admiringly. Dave had the knack of making the reporters feel grateful for those five minutes he'd allowed them for questions. Charisma was the word, she thought. Another officer could say the same thing and provoke resentment at it being such a short time.

Once the five minutes were up, Dave guided Yasmeen and Rachel from the room. He'd managed to field a few questions without giving away the fact that, in reality, the team were no nearer finding Ayesha than they had been the day she was taken.

Morven realised she needed to follow the DI to find out about the task he had planned for her. She managed to fight her way out of the room and hurried to

Dave's office where he was standing with Yasmeen Khalil and Rachel Roberts.

'Why do I need another officer following me around?' Yasmeen was saying. Her tone didn't sound like someone who had been sobbing inconsolably minutes earlier. 'I like Rachel. Why can't she stay with me?'

'We're only human, Mrs Khalil,' Dave said. 'Rachel has been on duty for more than two days without a break. I'm afraid I'll have to insist that she takes at least today off. PC Jennings is equally able to support you.'

Damned with faint praise, Morven thought, but made sure she kept her face impassive. It was clear now that her task for at least the next day or so was to be liaison officer for the Khalil family.

It was something she'd never done before but she understood the requirements of the role. She'd even done a short training course a few months earlier when Dave Bradley had decided that all his staff should be able to cover several roles.

She smiled at Yasmeen and held out her hand when Dave introduced her. But the training course hadn't prepared Morven for the look of hatred that flashed in Yasmeen Khalil's eyes as she kept her own hand firmly by her side.

6

While Yasmeen Khalil was giving a formal witness statement elsewhere in the building, Rachel Roberts quickly briefed Morven on what had happened over the past couple of days.

One of the more experienced officers on the team, Rachel had acted as family liaison officer on dozens of cases. Morven wanted to learn as much as she could about the Khalil family from her before she left for her well-earned break.

'She's a strange one, is our Mrs Khalil, that's for sure. All she did all weekend was sit looking out of the window of her apartment. She barely ate or drank and if she slept at all, then I must have dropped off too because I didn't notice.

'But the really odd thing is, well, I can't really put my finger on it, but she didn't seem to be expecting any word from the kidnappers. Other families I've worked with have sat staring at the phone. She didn't seem to expect hers to ring.'

Rachel gulped down the last of the mug of coffee Morven had made for her.

'And another thing. She didn't seem to want to talk about Ayesha. That's the other thing most parents of missing kids do. They go over and over things the child likes or does. As if they're trying to keep them close by telling you all about them. But not Yasmeen. Even when I tried to encourage her to talk about Ayesha she just didn't want to.

'I've been waiting for her to fall apart and I thought that was it just now in the press conference, but by the time we were up here she was back to normal. Anyway, over to you — and good luck.'

Rachel left, desperate to get home and rest.

Morven sat thinking about what

Rachel had told her for a few minutes. She wasn't sure she'd have picked up on those things as odd behaviour. She knew she still had a lot to learn from her more experienced colleagues.

The DI had told Morven to take a couple of hours to go home and pack a bag. Then he wanted her to come back and pick up Yasmeen Khalil, and move in with her and her husband, who should be at their apartment by now. Liaison officers don't usually move in with the family but there was something about this situation that didn't fit and Dave Bradley wanted someone on the inside.

It struck Morven that it was ridiculous to go back to her flat for her things, then all the way back to the station only to travel to an apartment next door to her own. However she couldn't deal with explaining why she lived in such an upmarket area. Keeping her home and work lives separate had become such a habit over the years that it was now as natural to her as breathing.

It was the instinct for self-preservation that stopped her inviting any of her colleagues round or even letting them know where she lived at all.

It could make her appear unfriendly, she knew that. Once when they'd been planning a team night out, one of her colleagues offered to pick her up but she fobbed them off by saying she had an errand to do on the way. It was the same when anyone offered her a lift home or to share a cab. It would only need one slip of the tongue for her to risk the identity it had taken her ten years to build.

She trusted her colleagues — you had to, in a job where you depended on each other to cover your back. But recent changes in the team had shown her that every organisation had its bad apples and she was determined not to let her personal life be threatened.

As she opened the front door she heard the TV blaring, which was odd. Surely Paula should be at college on a Monday morning. She could also hear the shower running in Paula's en-suite so maybe she was just running late.

Morven threw the essentials into a small trolley bag. She had plenty of time so she decided to grab an early lunch — she had no idea when her next meal would be.

She had just finished making a tuna sandwich when Paula walked into the room. Morven nearly dropped her glass of water.

'Your hair,' she said, eyebrows raised. 'It's very, er, different.'

'Don't you like it?' Paula asked. 'And what are you doing here anyway?'

Ignoring the first question, Morven explained that she would be away for a day or two for work. She couldn't take her eyes from Paula. She had dyed her beautiful auburn mop of hair. It was now dark brown and almost exactly the same colour as Morven's.

She knew it was none of her business what Paula chose to do to her appearance, but she thought it had been much nicer before.

Morven took her sandwich into the sitting room and switched off the TV. While she ate, she thought about the task ahead of her. It would be full-on but she was looking forward to the challenge. She was glad Dave Bradley was trusting her with something interesting at last.

She was also feeling a little anxious about how he might react if anything went wrong. But why should it? How hard could it be to stay with the kidnapped child's parents in their home?

As she popped the last piece of bread into her mouth, Morven's attention was taken by Paula's laptop which sat open on the table. Without really registering what she was doing she tapped the trackpad, bringing the screen to life.

She was only idly curious about whether Paula had been studying or playing games. After all, Morven had yet to see much evidence of Paula taking her studies seriously.

What she saw puzzled her. The screen was showing an acknowledgement of an order for contact lenses. Yet Paula had perfect vision. Even more strange, the lenses had a dark brown tint.

Morven had just got to her feet to take her plate and glass away when Paula dashed into the room, slammed the laptop shut and took it back to her bedroom.

Was it really only yesterday that I was relishing having Paula's company? Morven thought. Suddenly her feelings about having a flatmate were changing. But working out what Paula was up to would have to wait. She had a job to do.

* * *

When she got back to the station Dave Bradley and Yasmeen Khalil were waiting for her in the DI's office. She could tell Dave was eager to pack Yasmeen off home so he could get on with running the investigation. Babysitting anxious parents was a job he obviously considered more suitable for someone of a far lower rank.

'PC Jennings, you know the score. Stay with Mrs Khalil and if there's any contact from the kidnappers, alert us immediately.'

He was being abrupt but Morven didn't take it personally. She knew how much pressure he was under on this case.

'You can count on me, boss,' she said, cringing inwardly at her clichéd reply.

Yasmeen had apparently come to terms with the change of liaison officer. She hadn't spoken to Morven yet but at least the expression of sheer hostility had gone from her face.

The two women left the building and were picked up by a patrol car. The driver gave Morven a nod as they set off and within moments they were crawling through the traffic of the capital.

Yasmeen was silent for the whole car journey. Morven would have expected her to want to talk about what had happened to her child or to ask questions about the investigation. However she supposed everyone was different and this was Yasmeen's way of coping in an extreme situation.

Morven gave her own apartment

block a quick glance as they passed by and the driver dropped them at the front door of Windsor Towers. Yasmeen entered the code that allowed them into the lobby. As they waited for the lift, Yasmeen finally spoke.

'My husband's here already. He phoned me while I was at the police station. It's good that you're here with me. He blames me for what's happened. I don't know what he would do if I arrived home alone.'

All this was spilled out quickly and then she hung her head, apparently ashamed of having to admit it to Morven.

The lift arrived and they entered as Yasmeen continued, 'In our culture women are expected to behave very differently to here. We're rarely allowed out without our husbands. I love our visits here because I can have some freedom. Now Hamid will never let me out of his sight again.'

Morven was taken aback, but it wasn't anything she hadn't come across before. Her team worked on too many cases where domestic abuse and mis-treatment of women were involved. She'd never worked with an abused woman from another country, though.

Seeing Yasmeen so vulnerable made Morven feel guilty about her reaction earlier. Of course Yasmeen would be hostile to new people. She would find it hard to trust anyone if even her husband could be so cruel as to blame her for the kidnapping.

Morven was not looking forward to meeting Hamid Khalil at all.

* * *

John Whitehouse MP was at a lunch-time meeting with his electoral agent. Although it was probably a few years until the next election, he liked to work closely with the people who would organise his bid for re-election. They always met at a busy pub that did excellent food and also gave John the opportunity to meet lots of potential voters. He was always on duty, as he saw it, even at meal times.

However today he was struggling to keep his attention on what Robert Cross was saying. The press conference had gone well. The detective inspector in charge of the case had emphasised the seriousness of the situation and Yasmeen had come across as the helpless, devastated mother everyone expected to see.

The next part of the plan couldn't be carried out until later, so why couldn't he just relax and concentrate? He realised that Robert had asked him a question and was waiting for an answer.

'I'm sorry, Robert. What was that?'

'I just asked if you enjoyed the breakfast fundraiser last Friday,' Robert said. 'I'm sorry I couldn't be there but it went well by all accounts.'

'Oh, yes,' John said with a smile. 'I find it so rewarding being involved with the hospice. They weren't so sure a breakfast time event would be popular, but we raised even more than planned. Such a simple idea, too — a pop-up café serving up coffee and sandwiches to commuters. They're going to make it a regular monthly thing.'

John wished he could share with his agent exactly how beneficial to his image the Friday morning event had been. Talk about killing two birds with one stone — it had provided him with the perfect alibi, as well as being great PR. But of course he couldn't be entirely honest with Robert on this occasion.

'Well, the marketing people got loads of great publicity shots,' Robert said. 'They'll take pride of place in the hospice's new fundraising appeal and we can use some of them next time we print election leaflets.'

'That's good,' John said. He'd already seen the photos and deleted any that could have ruined the plan. He wouldn't be surprised if the police wanted to question him at some point and if they did he'd be able to show them dozens of pictures of himself at the south-west London hospice fundraiser. Let them try to prove he wasn't there.

* * *

As Yasmeen reached towards the keypad to enter the code that would give them access to the apartment, the door was suddenly yanked open. A wiry, dark-haired man stood in the doorway, his eyes blazing with anger. He reached out and grabbed Yasmeen by the wrist, dragging her across the threshold.

Before Morven could react he had slammed the door in her face. She was stunned. This hadn't been covered on the training course.

Within seconds she had pulled herself together and hammered on the door.

'Mr Khalil,' she shouted, not knowing whether her voice would carry through the thick wooden door. 'I'm a police officer. I'm here to support you and your wife.'

Morven knew her priorities had changed within the last few minutes. Rather than simply being the Khalils' liaison officer, she now knew that she had to protect Yasmeen from her own husband.

'Mr Khalil,' she tried again. 'I must insist that you open this door.' It sounded ridiculous, even to her own ears but, incredibly, a few seconds later the door opened a few inches.

'We don't need you,' Hamid Khalil said. 'Go out and find our daughter instead of wasting your time here.'

The door closed again and Morven slumped against the wall. She sighed as she realised that the one time Dave Bradley had picked her for a key task, she had failed.

It was all very well for Hamid Khalil to say they didn't need her, but baby-sitting the family was only one of the purposes of the family liaison officer. With close access they were often able to find evidence that would otherwise remain hidden. Unpleasant as it may be to face, it often turned out that the family themselves were involved in whatever crime had been committed.

Could that be why Hamid Khalil had turned her away? What did he have to hide?

No matter what the reason for Hamid's hostility was, Morven knew her immediate problem was that she needed to let the DI know what had happened. She'd been in trouble at the weekend for going straight to the detectives' team instead of her supervisor, Sergeant Foster. But this was different. Her task had been assigned to her directly by Dave Bradley.

She reached out her phone and selected him from her contacts list. Of course it went to voicemail. He was constantly busy from the moment he arrived at the station until he left. She'd leave a quick message and hope he got back to her soon.

'Hello, boss, it's Morven. PC Jennings.' She'd suddenly become nervous which was ridiculous, considering all she was doing was passing on some information to the senior investigating officer on the case. She cleared her throat and her voice sounded more normal as she continued, 'I've been prevented from entering the apartment by Hamid Khalil and I'm concerned for his wife's safety. I'll back off for now as he was quite, er, assertive. Please call back and advise how to proceed.'

There was nothing more Morven could do and since she was so close to home, she decided to go back and await the DI's phone call there.

She was feeling unsure about whether she had dealt with the situation correctly. Should she have waited outside the Khalils' door until she was perhaps eventually allowed in?

That would just be a waste of time and might have antagonised Hamid Khalil. He had made his feelings about her being there perfectly clear. There were no outstanding tasks she could complete if she headed back to the station, so she might as well call it a day until she received further instructions, she reasoned. It was one of the strangest working days she'd ever known.

It only took Morven a couple of minutes to walk to her own apartment block. Glancing back at Windsor Towers, she tried to work out which set of windows belonged to the Khalils' flat.

Counting up the floors, she realised that they were the penthouse flat of their block. Windsor Towers must be a couple of floors lower than her own block. It was difficult to get perspective when both blocks were so high.

She wondered if their views were as spectacular as hers, out over the landscape of London. But at the moment, every blind was closed in their windows. She hoped Yasmeen was OK.

Morven went up in the lift towards her own home. Hopefully by now Paula would have gone to college. But as she opened the door to the flat she heard voices coming from the sitting room.

Her heart sank. It was only a couple of hours earlier that she'd told Paula she would be away for a few days. It sounded as if she'd taken advantage of it to invite a guest round.

Morven thought back to the weekend, when she'd been thinking how good it was to have company. Now she was starting to think it was time to reclaim her space.

Walking into the sitting room, she stopped in her tracks.

'Ben?' she said. 'What are you doing here?'

'Oh, I was just passing,' Ben said cheerfully. 'Thought I'd drop in and check how my cousin was settling in.'

Morven frowned. This seemed wrong but she couldn't put her finger on why. Alarm bells were going off in her head, though. When Ben had suggested Paula could move in, Morven had wondered about a potential conflict of interest.

'Won't it compromise my witness protection?' she'd asked. 'It seems dangerous for me to get to know someone with family connections to you.'

'Not at all,' Ben had said. 'All Paula needs to know is that we're colleagues from work. Think about it — it's perfectly reasonable that a police officer and a witness protection officer would know each other. Plus, having someone I've known all her life means you don't need to worry about references.'

Since Paula had moved in, Morven had insisted on meeting Ben elsewhere if they needed to discuss anything to do with her witness protection status. She had believed Ben when he said there was no need for Paula to know that Morven was one of his clients, but it seemed more sensible for him not to come here. She was shocked and disappointed that he had apparently ignored her wishes. And seeing them here together, in her home, made Morven uncomfortable.

She stood, arms folded, until Ben got the message, gulped down the rest of his tea and headed for the door.

'I'll speak to you later, Paula,' he said. 'We can finish planning the surprise.'

'Surprise?' Morven asked after he'd left.

'Yeah — it's our grandma's seventieth birthday soon. We're planning a party.' Paula gathered up her things from the table and went to her bedroom. 'Oh, why are you back, by the way? I thought you said you'd be away for a while.'

'Things changed,' Morven said. She wasn't in the mood to chat to Paula. Now that the idea of having her flat to herself again had sneaked into her head, she was finding it hard to ignore. Once this case was finished, she'd put her mind to easing Paula out of her comfortable situation.

Trying to make use of the unexpected time at home, Morven got on with some domestic chores. As usual she avoided Paula's bedroom, deciding to give the sitting room a good going-over.

One of the advantages of being so well-off was being able to afford all the latest gadgets and her cordless vacuum cleaner was one of her favourites. Most of the rooms had wooden floors and she zipped round the sitting room in no time. She finished by cleaning under the coffee table and sofas and something caught her eye as she moved the table back into place.

Reaching down, she saw that it was a business card from her bank. On the back was written a date and time at the end of this week, presumably for an appointment.

Morven was puzzled. She did most of her banking online and hadn't been in to see her personal banker for ages. The card couldn't have been there long — her obsessive cleaning would have turned it up before now. No, it must have been in the pile of papers that Paula swept from the table earlier.

Morven's curiosity was aroused. Her bank wasn't just a normal high street branch. They catered for very rich clients.

She knocked on Paula's bedroom door but there was no response. Opening the door hesitantly, she saw the room was empty. Paula must have gone out while Morven was vacuuming.

Had she deliberately slipped out when she knew she wouldn't be heard? Morven could really do without this at home while she was working on an important case. The moment she thought that, her phone rang and she dashed to the kitchen where it was charging. The screen showed

Dave Bradley's number.

'Hi, Morven,' he said when she answered. 'I got your message. I've arranged for Hamid Khalil to be picked up and brought in to give a statement. That should give you a chance to get into the flat and check that his wife's all right. We'll speak later and decide whether you should stay there when he returns, OK?'

'Yes, that's fine,' Morven said, aware that she was enjoying speaking to Dave far too much to pretend that their relationship was simply professional. 'I'll get over there right away.'

'I should give it half an hour,' Dave said. 'Make sure Hamid's out of the way before you stroll down the road.'

So he knows where I live, Morven thought as they disconnected the call. She spent the half hour she had to kill tidying the kitchen surfaces and looking for other small jobs that were usually overlooked.

She kept glancing at Paula's door, a little voice telling her she could go in and have a quick look through her things. Maybe find out the explanation for that bank business card. But in the end she couldn't justify invading Paula's privacy.

There was, however, something she could do to quieten the worried voice that was telling her she should be suspicious of Paula. She quickly signed on to her computer and sent an email.

At last it was time to head to Windsor Towers. Morven took a last look round, pleased with the transformation she'd made in such a short time. She smiled to herself as she went down in the lift, knowing that in just a couple of minutes she'd be heading up almost as high in the next apartment block.

Morven rang the bell at the main entrance to Windsor Towers. It took a long while for Yasmeen to answer through the intercom. Morven knew she would be able to see her visitor on a small video screen.

'PC Jennings? What are you doing here?'

'My boss told me to come over while

your husband is at the station. Can you buzz me in, please?'

She heard a sigh and thought she heard a muffled voice and then the door buzzed.

When she arrived at the door of the flat the door opened a few inches and Yasmeen peered through. Morven wondered if she'd ever get the chance to see the inside of the apartment. She was starting to lose patience but, remembering her training, she kept calm and regulated her voice.

'Can you let me in, please, Mrs Khalil,' she said. 'I'm under orders to stay with you until your husband gets back.'

Maybe letting Yasmeen think she'd be in trouble if she didn't let her in would do the trick.

'I don't need you here, PC Jennings,' Yasmeen said. Her voice held an urgency that belied the words. 'My husband has just gone out for a short time. When he returns — you already know what he thinks of you being sent here. You might as well save yourself some time and leave now.'

Morven couldn't understand Yasmeen's attitude. Just a short while ago, she had been confiding in Morven about how her husband would blame her for their child's abduction. She had seemed afraid of Hamid Khalil so surely she would welcome Morven's company, especially once her husband returned. Something told her she needed to get into that apartment.

'Mrs Khalil, I strongly advise you to let me in and allow me to stay with you when your husband comes back.' Morven stood waiting, determined not to be turned away.

'You're not going to leave, are you?' Yasmeen said, shaking her head sadly as she opened the door.

Morven walked through, wondering why Yasmeen was looking so downhearted. Before she could think of any possible explanations, Morven felt a sharp scratch at the side of her neck. Her vision narrowed to a pinpoint as she slumped to the floor.

7

'Do I need a lawyer?' Hamid Khalil sat at the table in the interview room, the expression on his face giving the impression there was a bad smell in the room.

To be fair, that was highly likely as the previous interviewee didn't appear to have showered in weeks. Although the major crimes team had their own office, they had to share interview rooms with all the other teams based in the building.

'That's entirely up to you, Mr Khalil,' Dave Bradley said. 'I'm happy to wait while you arrange for your solicitor to attend. However, you're here simply to give a statement. It's standard procedure for us to interview all close family members. Your wife gave her statement earlier.'

Hamid quickly worked out that requesting his lawyer would delay matters considerably. A brief nod indicated that he was willing to proceed.

Half an hour later Dave left the room, wondering why he'd thought it would be useful for him to sit in. They were no wiser than they'd been before.

Hamid Khalil had been in Dubai for the past three months. When he was informed of his daughter's abduction he immediately made arrangements to travel to London, but this had not been possible until today. He had travelled on his uncle's private jet.

'Why didn't your wife and daughter use that jet instead of a commercial airline?' Dave had asked. He didn't add what he was thinking — that if Yasmeen and Ayesha Khalil had been travelling on the luxury jet they wouldn't have been in Heathrow's check-in hall and the abduction might never have happened.

'Her trip to London this time was unexpected,' Hamid said. 'She wanted to visit a sick friend. The privilege of using my uncle's plane is only offered when I am travelling with her.'

Unbelievable, Dave thought as he went back to his office.

* * *

Elly Clarke was sitting in the back of her dad's car as he drove her and her mum back from the restaurant.

This is it, she thought — *pure happiness.*

The family had been celebrating Elly's sixteenth birthday at her favourite Italian restaurant a few miles from their home. The highlight of the evening was when all the waiters had gathered round, one of them carrying a birthday cake with a sparkler candle, and they all sang 'Happy Birthday' to her.

Elly knew she was a bit weird, preferring to spend her birthday evening with her parents rather than with a gang of other teenage girls. Yet she didn't care. She had plenty of friends at school but none that she'd really call a best mate. She was happiest in her own company or spending time with her mum. When Dad had time, he tried to join in with their interests but the mother-daughter bond was definitely strongest.

They'd spent most of the evening planning their next holiday. Dad was going to hire a boat and they were going to sail around the islands off the west coast of Scotland.

People never understood why, when they were so well off, they didn't take more glamorous holidays. However they enjoyed keeping things simple more than showing off how rich they were. They'd spent their most recent holiday cycling and camping in Ireland and had a wonderful time.

Elly's dad had been a bit preoccupied since they came home, though. A couple of times her parents had been deep in conversation and then stopped talking abruptly when Elly walked in. She'd asked her mum about it but Eva Clarke had just brushed it off as nothing serious. And it certainly hadn't spoilt her birthday celebration.

As Dad pulled into the wide driveway to their house he frowned.

'Didn't you leave the outside lights on, darling?' he asked.

'I thought so, but it was light when we set off so I might have forgotten.' Mum peered out of the side window.

'Stay here while I check everything's OK,' Dad said. Turning round to look at Elly he tried to replace his worried expression with a smile. 'Don't worry, Elly, it'll be fine.'

Elly grinned back at him.

Ten years on, Morven could feel that smile on her face as she slowly climbed back into consciousness. She felt a few seconds of confusion. She was in the back seat of a large car but that was where the similarity between her current situation and her apparent dream ended.

Her wrists were tied together with the kind of plastic ties people use for gardening. She knew there was no use trying to loosen the ties. The more she struggled, the tighter they would become. She moved her feet slightly, relieved to find that her ankles weren't secured.

Morven's head was swimming. She realised she must have been drugged at Yasmeen's apartment. Her brain was still too fuzzy to try and work out why. She let her eyes scan the interior of the vehicle, though simply moving her eyes brought on a bout of nausea and dizziness.

It appeared to be a people carrier. There was a broad-shouldered man sitting in the front passenger seat but apart from the fact he had very short fair hair, she couldn't see anything of his appearance. Ah — she could see the driver's eyes reflected in the rear view mirror.

A familiar spark of recognition hit her, the same as when she identified a suspect on CCTV. She knew those eyes. She just needed to think calmly and allow her memory banks to deliver up a name.

A few moments later it hit her. He was the detective who'd been kicked out of the force the previous month.

What on earth was going on?

Morven was sure she'd heard that Matt Hanlon had gone into private security as a bodyguard. This felt like trying to put together a jigsaw without the picture. None of the pieces of information seemed to fit.

Finally Morven's eyes rested on the person at the other end of the back seat. Yasmeen Khalil was slumped with her head resting against the window. Had she been drugged too?

Possibly — but her wrists weren't tied so Morven decided it was more likely that Yasmeen was a voluntary passenger and had simply given in to exhaustion at last.

Morven's head was much clearer now, but part of her wished she could have stayed oblivious to the danger she was in. On the positive side, she was still alive. If these two men had wanted to harm her they could have done so already, rather than have the hassle of tying her up and loading her into the car.

But while she had no idea what was going on, Morven still felt vulnerable. She forced herself to focus on all the facts she knew about the Khalils. There must be a clue somewhere to what she had stumbled onto.

Just before she had been drugged, Yasmeen had tried to get her to go away. Morven assumed that Yasmeen had been about to leave with the two men. It wasn't too far a leap to guess that this was connected to Ayesha's kidnapping.

Yet it didn't make sense. The pattern of any other abductions she'd heard about was that the kidnappers would contact the family soon after the abduction to demand a ransom. In this case it had been more than three days since Ayesha was taken and there had been no contact at all.

Eventually Morven gave up trying to work out what was going on. Her head was thumping with pain from the drugs and from dehydration. She had no idea how long they'd been on the road and of course she didn't have a clue what their destination would be.

For someone used to being in control, this was a nightmare. For now, she decided the most sensible thing to do was copy Yasmeen and try to get some rest. Now all she needed to do was convince her racing mind to switch off. Whatever was waiting for her at the end of this journey, she would need her wits about her.

* * *

After he left the Hamid Khalil interview Dave Bradley took stock of what still needed doing before he could call it a day. He was about to draft a quick update email for his boss when he remembered that he should have called Morven Jennings back to discuss whether she should stay at the Khalils' home once Hamid returned.

Having spent some time in Hamid's company he felt a bit guilty about dropping Morven into the situation. However it would be good experience, and he knew she could do it. Regardless of his romantic thoughts about Morven, he recognised a good police officer when he met one.

He tried Morven's number but it went straight to voicemail so her phone must be either busy or switched off. He left a quick message simply asking her to ring back when she could.

Half an hour later he was catching up on some paperwork when one of the detective constables shouted through his open office door.

'Boss, I've got Hamid Khalil on the line. He's demanding to speak to you.'

Sighing, Dave picked up the phone when the DC had transferred the call.

'Bradley,' he said sharply. 'What can I do for you, Mr Khalil?'

He was trying to keep the impatience from his voice, but he'd seen the man less than an hour ago. What could he possibly want? If he was going to make a complaint about PC Jennings being at his home, Dave wouldn't put up with it.

This guy seemed to think the police

were his servants, waiting around to do as he told them. Well, he might call the shots back at his Dubai training stables but here he was just another person with a home in the Met Police's area. Dave believed in treating them all equally. But when Hamid Khalil spoke, the panic in his voice made Dave pay close attention.

'DI Bradley. I've just got home and my wife isn't here. She wouldn't have gone out alone willingly. What can have happened to her?'

'Calm down, Mr Khalil,' Dave said. 'PC Jennings should have been with your wife. Perhaps they've gone somewhere together.'

'That young girl?' Hamid answered. Dave could almost hear the sneer in the contemptuous tone. 'What could she do to protect Yasmeen? Anyway, you don't understand. The front door was wide open and it looks as if there was a struggle.'

'Right, I'm sending some officers over now,' Dave said. The usual procedure for a missing person didn't apply here. A police officer was involved and the Khalils' child had already been abducted. 'Don't touch anything.'

He slammed the phone down and looked out into the main office to see who was still at their desk and picked two people to go straight over to Windsor Towers, first telling them to request a CSI team to meet them there. Then he sat back in his chair and tried to get his head around what Hamid had told him.

At the forefront of his mind was the dread of something happening to Morven, but his professional brain soon kicked in and he started to think logically. From the scene Hamid had described, it sounded as if Yasmeen Khalil had been taken from her apartment by force. The fact that Dave had been unable to contact Morven suggested that she might have been taken too.

Why did nobody seem to have landline phones any more? he wondered. If he'd been able to phone Morven's home, he could at least have confirmed whether or not she had gone to Windsor Towers. She might have been delayed at home . . .

He realised he was clutching at straws. The only way to find out whether she had left her apartment was to go there. Since it was so close to the crime scene he needed to visit, he would have no trouble justifying a quick trip to Morven's home on the way.

* * *

The traffic was mercifully lighter than usual so Dave reached Morven's apartment block more quickly than he'd expected. He raised an eyebrow as he approached the front entrance. He'd known it was an upmarket area but everything about the place screamed money.

He pressed the buzzer for the penthouse apartment, praying that Morven would answer. He wouldn't care what excuse she made for not following orders — he just wanted her safe.

But when the intercom crackled into

life it wasn't Morven's voice.

'Hi, who is it?' the chirpy female voice said.

'Hello, it's Detective Inspector Bradley. I'm looking for Morven Jennings.'

'The famous DI Bradley?' the voice squealed. 'Come on up.'

The door buzzed open. Waiting for the lift, Dave wondered about the words he'd just heard. 'The famous DI Bradley'. So Morven obviously talked about him outside work. *In a good way or a bad way?* he wondered.

The fact that someone else lived here might answer the mystery of how Morven could afford to live in such a place. A rich relative, maybe? He knew how much police constables earned and it was nowhere near enough to be able to buy or even rent a home like this.

Paula was waiting at the front door of the apartment when Dave got out of the lift.

'You're going to think I'm such an idiot,' she said. 'I should have told you Morven isn't here.'

Dave's heart sank.

'It's OK. I would've needed to come up and speak to you anyway. Are you related? Sisters, perhaps?'

As he asked the question, he looked closely at Paula. Although her hair was the same colour as Morven's, her most striking feature made a family relationship unlikely. While Morven's eyes were dark brown, this woman had the most piercing blue eyes Dave had ever seen. As if a sapphire and a diamond had merged to form glittering deep-blue gems.

'No.' Paula laughed. 'We're just flatmates. Paula Gill.' She held out her hand and Dave shook it.

Paula could understand Morven's infatuation with this guy. He was physically attractive, there was no denying it, but it was more than that. His whole demeanour was striking and magnetic. But she needed to remember that first and foremost he was a senior police officer.

For a moment Paula feared he would be able to read her thoughts and know what she was planning. She had to pull herself together and concentrate on what he was here for.

'Do you know what time Morven left?' he asked. He was still hoping against hope that she hadn't been at the Khalils' apartment by the time Yasmeen had apparently been abducted. Still, he knew if that was the case she would have shown up by now.

'I'm not sure. She came back to do some cleaning up and I had to go out before she left again. I came home about twenty minutes ago and she'd gone by then.'

Paula had slipped out of the apartment while Morven was doing her obsessive vacuuming. She'd taken the chance to get out of the way so she could avoid any awkward questions from Morven, and it had worked. By the time she came back she had the place to herself.

So there was no way of working out exactly when she'd gone out, Dave thought. They'd have to assume she was now with Yasmeen Khalil. That they'd both been abducted.

With a sigh he thanked Paula and left, assuring her he'd keep her updated about Morven. Although he hadn't gone much further in than the hallway of the apartment, Dave had noticed the tasteful, expensive-looking decor. It all added to the mystery of Morven's living arrangements and how she could afford them.

For now, Dave pushed that to the back of his mind. His priority was finding Morven. And Mrs Khalil and her child, of course. But more and more Dave Bradley was realising just how much Morven meant to him. What was that saying?

You don't know what you've got 'til it's gone.

Dave left his car parked by the road and walked across to Windsor Towers. He made a promise to himself. He would find Morven and then he would make sure she was kept safe forever.

* * *

Paula managed to keep the sickly smile on her face until the lift door had closed and DI Bradley was on his way down to the ground floor. Then she slammed the apartment door and ran to find her phone. Her call was answered on the first ring and she was relieved — this call couldn't wait.

'We need to bring things forward,' she said, as calmly as she could.

'Why? What's changed?'

'Morven's boss has just been here. He reckons she's gone missing. She's working on that baby kidnapping that's been on the news. He wasn't giving much away but he has no idea where Morven is.'

It took the other person a moment to realise the implications of what Paula was saying.

'Can we change the appointment at the bank — bring it forward?'

'I'll ring them the minute they open in the morning and tell them I'm going in. They're hardly going to turn away one of their best customers, are they?'

'What about all the computer stuff?'

'I've done all the preparation,' Paula said. 'There won't be any problem with that. There's only one thing bothering me. I ordered the contact lenses online, guaranteed next day delivery, but I don't know what time they'll arrive tomorrow.'

'Well, let's hope they come early. You might not pull it off otherwise. But I don't think that's the only thing that should be bothering you. You realise, don't you, that if Morven's really disappeared our whole plan could be ruined? Make that call to the bank first thing — and Paula?'

'Yes?' Paula asked.

'Do not mess this up. You know how much depends on you giving a convincing performance.'

Paula ended the call. She knew that last comment was true. The whole plan depended on her being able to look enough like her flatmate to convince the bank staff she was indeed Morven.

They'd done their research well and

knew that Morven's usual personal banker was on holiday this week. If they had to postpone, and the usual member of staff returned, who knew how long it would be before they got another chance?

If Morven really had gone missing, if she never turned up, all their months of planning would be wasted. No, their best hope was to go ahead tomorrow. Paula wouldn't let herself dwell on the possibility of failure so she convinced herself that the police wouldn't release personal details of a missing officer by then.

Paula didn't know how long she could carry on pretending to be a student when she wasn't even enrolled at a college. More importantly, she didn't know how long she could carry on playing best friends with Morven while planning to steal a large chunk of her fortune.

It wasn't that Paula was having any pangs of conscience but the longer she'd lived with Morven, the more aware she had become of the other woman's intelligence and intuition. Paula was no longer sure her acting skills were up to this job.

Paula spent the rest of the afternoon and evening putting the finishing touches to everything she needed for the following day. If there hadn't been so much depending on her success at the bank, Paula might have enjoyed trying on all Morven's clothes and experimenting with her make-up.

When she was finally satisfied that the only thing missing was the contact lenses, she called it a day and went to bed. With such a big day ahead, most people might find it hard to fall asleep, but Paula never had any trouble sleeping. As soon as her head touched the pillow she fell into a deep, dreamless slumber.

At home on the outskirts of the city, it was well into the early hours before her partner in crime finally snatched a couple of hours' sleep.

* * *

John Whitehouse was pacing the floor of his brother's kitchen. He'd driven over to Newmarket in record time, desperate to escape London and all its current pressures. Everything seemed to be spiralling out of control. It should have been so simple.

Whitehouse was used to things running smoothly. He was used to things going his way. Disrupted plans were a new experience for him and he didn't like it. He didn't like it at all.

His brother, Mark, came back in from his evening check of the horses. He took one look at John and reached down a half-full bottle of scotch.

John stopped his pacing and the brothers sat down at the large wooden table that dominated the room. They both downed their first drink quickly and Mark refilled their glasses.

'So come on then, bro,' he said. 'Tell me what trouble you've got me into this time.'

It had been a pattern throughout their lives. Mark was the steady older brother, always destined to follow in their father's footsteps. John, just a couple of years younger, outshone Mark academically and had no interest in the family business. He loved racing for the spectacle and the networking opportunities it offered. But the life of a racehorse trainer was too much like hard work for him.

At school, if ever there was a hint of trouble for John, Mark would step in, either to take the blame or to defend John. That carried on into adulthood. John had Mark to thank for his being able to stand as a member of parliament.

A handful of minor offences over the years would have put paid to his dreams had Mark not stepped in to admit to them. His logic was that he only ever planned to work in the family business so, as long as they were only petty crimes, it wouldn't affect him. If anything had threatened his chances of getting a training licence, of course that would have been a different matter.

So last week when John had phoned Mark and asked him to give up his Friday morning to impersonate him at a charity event, Mark had agreed unquestioningly. His assistant would relish the chance to run the place alone for a morning. He assumed John had just double-booked himself and didn't want to let the charity down.

Although they weren't twins the resemblance between the brothers was strong enough to fool anyone but friends and family — none of whom would be at the hospice event. It was only now, seeing the agitated state his brother was in, that Mark began to suspect there was something seriously wrong.

They were too old now to shrug off the way John avoided his responsibilities. He was an MP, for goodness' sake. And Mark himself had built up quite a reputation. If John had dragged him into something that could threaten the stables, he didn't know how he would ever forgive him. This was their father's legacy.

Looking round the kitchen, Mark remembered so many happy times spent in this room. Both boys had been too young when their mother died to really remember her at all. Their dad had basically brought them both up alone and his way of showing his love for them was by involving them in the life and work of the stables.

He didn't believe in showing favouritism to his boys and they had to start at the bottom, mucking out and doing whatever jobs the stable lads found for them. It was hard work, seven days a week, that they had to fit in around their school work.

For Mark, this was wonderful because it was all he ever wanted to do. He would race home after school and head for his favourite horses, helping the stable lads to groom and generally look after them. In the school holidays he would spend all day there, watching the training gallops and helping to get horses ready for their trips to the races. If he was really lucky he'd be allowed to travel with one of the horsebox teams and actually spend the day at the racecourse.

But for John, who hated the day-to-day life of the stables, it felt like a punishment to be sent to help. The only time he enjoyed it was when he, too, was allowed to travel for a day out at the races. But over time his trips dwindled because the stable lads complained that he wouldn't help them — he just wanted a free day out.

As the boys grew older this difference between them started to affect their relationship with their father. He was bound to show more affection to the child who wanted to follow in his footsteps. But to give him his due, he tried very hard to get on with John too. Any new hobby John showed an interest in would be indulged.

When he decided he wanted to start a band with his school friends his dad bought him a top of the range guitar, then a keyboard and then a drum kit. But John didn't stick to trying to learn any of them for more than a few months.

That became the pattern for his whole life. The only thing he had ever stuck to was being a politician.

Sadly, their father had died before John achieved his success by being elected to parliament.

Mark, though, had been proud of his brother for achieving his goal. He would never dream of telling his little brother but every week he recorded Prime Minister's Questions on the Parliament Channel and tried to spot John on screen. He was obviously popular in his constituency, judging by the number of people who had come to shake Mark's hand, thinking he was John, last week at the hospice event. It had looked as if John might have turned a corner and might actually be making some sensible life choices at last.

Until now. Something had clearly gone very wrong.

'Come on, John. Tell me.'

John looked into his brother's eyes and began to explain.

8

Morven had been lulled into an uneasy sleep again but thankfully, this time she was spared dreaming about the night her parents died.

She had been plagued by the dreams for years. If she was lucky, it was the pleasant dream about her sixteenth birthday celebration. She always woke with a smile from that one. But more often it was the dream that followed on from their return home from the birthday meal.

Morven's father left her and her mum in the car while he went to check the house. The headlights lit his path as he approached the front door. Morven, or Elly as she was then, watched as he reached the house. She knew there was something wrong when he pushed the door open without needing to use his key.

Seconds later there was a flash of light in the hallway and a loud bang. Elly's mum was out of the car and running towards the house before Elly could scream at her to stop. She didn't even make it inside before the gunman stopped her with another shot.

Elly was paralysed with shock and fear. That's what saved her life as she sat frozen in the back seat of the car. The gunman glanced in her direction but the headlights must have prevented him seeing her as their glare dazzled his eyes.

The image of the killer's face was imprinted on Elly's brain. He was wearing a black balaclava but she could see his steely grey eyes and long, straight nose. Those were the features Morven had been searching for ever since she became a super recogniser.

He had disappeared by the time Elly managed to force herself to get out of the car. She stumbled to where her mother lay, then went into the house, sobbing, because she knew there was nothing she could do to save her mum.

One look at her dad was enough to tell her was beyond help too.

Crying uncontrollably, she managed to phone 999. Then she sat on the stairs with her head in her hands.

Her childhood ended that night when she swore to herself that she would see justice for her parents. Everyone told her how brave and grown-up she was, but she knew that there was no alternative. She was on her own now.

Once it sank in that her parents were gone forever, her biggest fear was that she would have to go into care. Fortunately her parents' wills had planned ahead for her being left an orphan, though they could never have imagined the horrific circumstances.

Although she had no blood relatives, a guardian had been named for her.

James Clarke and Adam McLean had been best friends since their schooldays. But while James had always been impatient to use his entrepreneurial skills, Adam was more academically minded.

When Adam achieved his ambition of

graduating from one of the top law schools in the USA and came home to set up his own law practice, it was natural that James would become his first client. It was a partnership that lasted right up until James and Eva Clarke's deaths. No one was surprised that Adam was named as guardian to Elly.

Adam and his wife took Elly into their home and cared for her in the immediate aftermath of the murders. She had known them all her life and even called them Aunt and Uncle. She would always be grateful to them for caring for her at that terrible time, and over the years one of her biggest regrets was that being in witness protection meant she could no longer contact them.

When it became clear that her parents' killer was not going to be found quickly it was Uncle Adam who had requested that Elly should be taken into the witness protection programme.

In the days following the murders it had become public knowledge that Elly had witnessed the killings. Her guardian was concerned that this might make her a target. In partnership with the witness protection service he made arrangements for her inheritance to be transferred into her new name. The meeting at which this was finalised was the last time she saw him.

The next couple of years were spent transforming Elly Clarke into Morven Jennings. The closest thing she had to family at that time was her liaison officer, Jenny Mason.

They got along well right from their first meeting when they were trying to choose a new name for Elly. She'd always loved the name Morven so that was easy, but the surname was proving difficult. Jennings ended up being chosen because Morven liked the fact it was similar to Jenny.

'A permanent link for us when you finally ditch me from your caseload,' she joked.

'Hey, you might be challenging but you're the easiest case I've got, kid,' Jenny replied.

In recent months Morven had been missing Jenny terribly. She knew their relationship wasn't meant to be so close, and her temporary replacement Ben was OK, but there was a bond between Morven and Jenny that had taken ten years to build. You couldn't replace that easily.

There were several theories about the motive for her parents' murders. In the end, the one the police were convinced was true was that it was related to a business deal her father was involved in. He had apparently uncovered some illegal activity and had threatened to take evidence of it to the authorities.

He had kept the proof in the safe in his office at the family home, but when the house was searched the safe was found to be empty. He hadn't shared the information with anyone because he wasn't sure who he could trust. It was a dead end, and the police had eliminated all other leads. The case was still open.

When Morven had started work at the Met she had thought about trying to gain access to the files but she knew that would be risking losing her job. Instead she carried on, hoping that one day the man she had seen illuminated by car headlights on a dark driveway would appear on one of the CCTV files she reviewed as the main part of her job.

And what would she do, if and when that day came? The rational part of her said she would report him to someone who could resurrect her parents' case from the back burner. However there was a small part of her that would be tempted to take the law into her own hands.

Now, ten years on from the worst night of her life, Morven was jolted awake when the people carrier came to a halt in another dark driveway. Her eyes sprang wide open as, for a second, she couldn't work out what was happening. Her tied wrists soon reminded her.

The driver and front passenger got out of the car and the passenger went round the other side and opened the rear door. Yasmeen took off her seat belt, got out of the car and walked towards the large house with the two men. None of them even acknowledged that Morven was there.

However she had managed to get a good look at the male passenger, confirming what she had been starting to suspect earlier. He was Pete Harris, the other officer who had been transferred from the team a month ago. But rather than being kicked off the force completely he'd been sent back into uniform.

Morven felt slightly better for knowing who her two abductors were, though she had no idea why. Perhaps she felt they were less likely to harm her because they knew her.

So even though her legs weren't tied, she didn't make any attempt to escape from the car. She decided her best course of action was to be passive and do exactly what her captors demanded. She would play it by ear and try to reason with them later.

* * *

Mark Whitehouse still sat at his kitchen table with an untouched glass of scotch in front of him. His brother's revelations had left him stunned. But in the end he had no choice other than to go along with what John had suggested.

He didn't like it. Not one bit. But having done John the favour of impersonating him last Friday morning, he was in this up to his neck.

Nobody would believe that he hadn't been aware of the reason for him taking John's place at the hospice event. How could his brother have put him in this position? OK, so John's original plan had been relatively harmless, but it had still been illegal. And although John couldn't have predicted the tragic consequences, nevertheless he had still ploughed on with his crazy scheme.

Mark looked at the glass of scotch again. He'd already had two while listening to John get everything off his chest earlier. He poured this glassful down the sink. He was going to need a clear head.

A dozen different thoughts were competing for attention in his head. His top priority, of course, were his horses and the stable staff. The start of the flat racing season was only weeks away and it was one of the busiest times of the year at the stables.

He had been adamant with John. He would help him by putting his home at his disposal, but John's actions must not jeopardise the working life of the stables.

John had assured him everything would be fine and then gone off to make arrangements. Mark was reminded of why John was so successful as a politician. He had a way of making people agree to things that they knew, deep down, were wrong.

Mark's face took on a grim expression as he thought back to another time the consequences of John's actions had been devastating.

Mark's wife had never liked John. She had begged Mark to sever the family ties that made him constantly dance to John's tune, but Mark had resisted. No matter what, they were brothers.

There hadn't been one catastrophic event that had made her decide to leave him. It had been the countless 'little favours' over months and years that had built up. Finally she had issued an ultimatum warning him that if he carried on being at John's beck and call she would leave.

Mark couldn't even remember now what it was that had turned out to be the straw that broke the camel's back. He just knew that when he returned from a day at Ascot races she was no longer there. No amount of begging or pleading would convince her to come home and it wasn't long before the solicitor's letter arrived informing him of divorce proceedings.

The business was only just beginning to recover from the financial settlement he'd been forced to agree to.

Up until today that had been the worst experience of Mark's life — but having sat and listened to John telling him what he had done, Mark realised that things were about to get a whole lot worse. Yet even now, Mark had found himself agreeing to whatever John wanted.

Minutes after John had left the room, a small car had pulled up on the drive. Mark looked out of the window and saw John welcoming the driver, a young woman, who reached into the back seat of the car. She handed the precious cargo she had brought to John, emptied several bags from the car's boot and then drove away.

Typical, Mark thought. *John was so sure I'd do anything for him, he'd already told her to come here before he even asked me.*

* * *

DI Dave Bradley only spent a few minutes at the Khalils' apartment. The surroundings were as opulent as those in Morven's apartment block. Considering the Khalils only spent a few weeks a year here, they had certainly spent a fortune on decorating the place.

The CSIs had arrived ahead of him and were still collecting evidence from the area around the front door. Hamid Khalil was in his kitchen drinking tea but he didn't offer Dave a cup. Dave could understand that Hamid was angry about the lack of progress in finding his baby daughter and now, added to that, his wife had disappeared.

'We're working on the assumption that Mrs Khalil and my officer are together,' Dave said. 'PC Jennings will be doing everything she can to keep your wife safe.'

'Forgive me if I don't take much comfort from that,' Hamid said.

Dave looked at the other man and felt some compassion for him. At the same time, he had to keep in mind that Hamid could be involved in whatever had happened.

At times his job required the skills of a peace negotiator more than of a police officer. He needed to gain Hamid's trust somehow so that he would relax and might give himself away — if he was indeed involved.

Yet all Dave's experience of dealing with every kind of criminal character told him that Hamid was blameless in this. Dave was ninety percent sure Hamid was a victim rather than a rogue.

Fatigue was starting to mess with his head but he decided to follow his instincts and try to befriend Hamid. It couldn't do any harm to the investigation — and it might even make things easier if Hamid was on their side.

'Do you mind if I sit down?' he asked.

Hamid shrugged and Dave sat beside him at the kitchen table.

'We know very little at this stage,' he said. 'But you have my word I will keep you updated at all times. Here's my number.' He handed a business card to Hamid. 'Call me any time. I'm off back to the station now and my team will be working through the night.'

Dave got up and placed a hand on Hamid's shoulder, half expecting the other man to flinch from the touch. Instead he simply sat still.

'I know we didn't exactly get off on the right foot, Mr Khalil.'

'Hamid, please.'

'OK — Hamid. I hope you understand that we have to follow procedures. But I know you must be going through hell — and believe me, I do know something of how you're feeling.'

'Thank you,' Hamid said. His tough exterior showed signs of cracking. 'Now please, I'll be happier when I know you're back doing your job.'

The two men shook hands and Dave stopped for a brief word with the leader of the CSI team before leaving the apartment.

When he arrived back at his car, Dave sat for a few minutes before turning the key in the ignition. He'd meant what he said. He did know something of the anguish Hamid Khalil was feeling.

The depth of his own feelings had taken him by surprise, and his fears for Morven's safety were threatening to affect his objectivity on this case.

For a fleeting moment he considered requesting a meeting with his boss and discussing a possible conflict of interest. Then he came to his senses as he realised that his connection with Morven was all in his own head.

He drove back to the station with the prospect of snatching a few hours' sleep on the sofa in the coffee lounge. At least he'd remembered to phone Anne and ask her to bring a new supply of clean shirts and underwear for him to keep in his locker. He had no idea when he'd see his own home again.

He wasn't sure how he would have coped these past few months without Anne's help. Whether it was fetching things to the station for him or picking him up after a long shift when he felt too tired to face a long drive, she was always there for him. If he could remember later and find a few minutes, he would ask his assistant to organise some flowers for her.

* * *

It was about twenty minutes before anyone came out to the car to fetch Morven. She'd started to wonder whether she was destined to be taken somewhere else, but at last a figure approached the car.

Pete Harris looked slightly shamefaced as he opened the door and reached over to undo Morven's seatbelt. She was tempted to speak to him — ask him what was going on — but she stuck to her planned silence and apparent co-operation.

'You weren't meant to be mixed up in this,' he said quietly. As he spoke, he glanced over his shoulder to make sure Matt Hanlon wasn't in earshot. It was clear who was in charge.

Morven nodded to acknowledge his attempt to explain, then got out of the car, walking ahead of Harris as they went towards the house. The building was a large, brick-built house. Most of the windows were in darkness but some of the upper rooms had lights showing through open curtains. Morven had no idea where they were but it looked like a well-maintained home.

As they walked through the front door Pete Harris nudged Morven towards the stairs and they climbed up. The door nearest the top of the stairs was open and he told her to go in.

It was a long room that seemed to take up a large part of the upper floor at the front of the house. It took a moment for Morven's eyes to adjust to the light, then she blinked a couple of times, trying to make sense of what she was seeing.

At the far end of the room, on a blue sofa, Yasmeen Khalil sat. She was hugging a small child tightly.

Ayesha? It must be, but Morven took a moment to realise what this meant.

Yasmeen had travelled here voluntarily, not tied up and drugged like Morven. Either the two men had threatened to harm Ayesha if her mother didn't come with them . . . or Yasmeen herself was involved in the child's abduction.

Something else was niggling at Morven's brain. Something that didn't fit at all. A second later, it came to her.

It would be simple to assume that the two men who had driven them here tonight, her former colleagues Hanlon and Harris, were the ones who had kidnapped Ayesha. But Morven had viewed the abduction on Heathrow's CCTV many times. Had it been these two, she would have recognised them immediately. You didn't have to be a super recogniser to know two colleagues you had worked with for months. The Heathrow suspects were still unidentified.

Morven tried to focus on her present predicament rather than struggling to work out how Ayesha's abduction had been carried out. There would be time enough for that later, she hoped, as long as she kept her wits about her and managed to get out of here safely.

'Sit there,' Pete Harris said, more brusquely than he had spoken to her before. Scared of looking soft in front of Hanlon, Morven realised. She sat on the upright chair he had pointed to and Harris produced a length of nylon rope. Within seconds he had tied her to the chair around her waist and used two smaller ropes to secure her ankles to the chair legs. With her wrists still being tied, she was now unable to move apart from being able to turn her head.

'It's just for now,' Harris whispered. 'When Hanlon's gone I'll come back up and let you off the chair.'

Morven didn't know what Harris was trying to achieve with his attempts at being kind to her. When this was all over, the boss would throw the book at Harris and Hanlon and it would make no difference that Harris had said a few kind words to Morven.

She tried to keep her face impassive so that he wouldn't see the contempt she felt for him. There were few things worse than a police officer gone bad. She consoled herself with the thought of him and Harris being sent to prison and the welcome that would await them. Former police officers were only one step higher than people who'd harmed children once they were in prison.

Hanlon and Harris left the room after a short whispered conversation. As the door closed, there was the sound of a key being turned in the lock.

Morven turned her head and stared at Yasmeen Khalil. Ayesha had fallen asleep and Yasmeen was settling her into a travel cot next to the sofa.

Morven waited until she had sat down again.

'Yasmeen, you need to tell me what's going on,' she said.

Yasmeen wouldn't make eye contact. She was plucking at a loose thread on the sofa and her breathing became more rapid before she finally answered.

'I'm so sorry,' she said. 'I tried to make you go away but you wouldn't listen. They said we couldn't hang around while I tried to get rid of you. I didn't know they were going to drug you.'

'So why had they come prepared with a syringe of God knows what?'

Morven said. 'Never mind that for now, I'm more interested in why you didn't need drugging. You don't seem very surprised to have been reunited with your daughter. Have you been in on it all along?'

Yasmeen was silent for a minute. Morven could almost see the internal struggle she was going through reflected on her face. At last she looked Morven directly in the eye and sighed.

'We could be here for a while,' she said. 'Let me tell you a story.'

9

The sun was just starting to show itself over the river when Dave Bradley woke up. Glancing at his watch, he worked out that he'd managed about four hours' sleep.

Not bad, and not much less than he usually had at home. When he tried to get up, though, he realised the main advantage that home had over the coffee lounge at the police station. He had a crick in his neck and his back felt as if he'd been sleeping on a park bench.

I'm getting too old for this, he thought, then laughed at the idea of thirty being too old.

Maybe he should go for promotion after all. He never saw his senior officers here outside office hours. They were always at the end of the phone in case of important developments but they didn't actually have to be here.

He went through to the locker room and retrieved a change of clothes. Ten minutes later he was showered, shaved and dressed and nobody would have been able to guess where he had spent the night. This was what made it worth it — the chance to jump straight back into work without having to battle through traffic on the commute first.

A couple of people were already at their desks, though from the look of their tired faces Dave wasn't sure if they were in early or still there from the previous night. He made a mental note to praise them for their commitment.

His job wasn't just about the case. He was a people manager too, and a lot of his job satisfaction came from encouraging and developing the talents of his staff.

For now, he made coffees and brought them through to their desks, stopping for a quick chat before going to his office.

Dave wanted to organise his thoughts before the team briefing that would start shortly. There wouldn't be much to add to the message he had sent to the whole team the previous evening.

He'd wanted them all to know immediately that Morven Jennings was missing, as was Yasmeen Khalil. There had been a flurry of replies about Morven. She was more popular than she realised and everyone was concerned about her disappearance.

The CSI team had found nothing to give the major crime team any leads. This whole case had been a series of dead ends. They would proceed on the assumption that Yasmeen Khalil and Morven had been taken by the same people as Ayesha Khalil. It was too much of a coincidence for their disappearance to be unconnected.

Since they had no clue as to Ayesha's whereabouts, that didn't really help. They were now into day four after Ayesha's abduction. The press were already hinting at police incompetence despite the media team's attempts to keep them onside. They would have a field day when they found out that not only was the child's mother missing but a police officer too.

On the bright side, once Dave had briefed his boss on their lack of progress, there'd be very little of him left for the press to take to pieces. He groaned at the prospect of the next couple of hours, then immediately felt guilty. However bad his morning might be, it was nothing compared to what Morven might be going through.

Determined to have something more to tell his boss than the bare fact that Mrs Khalil and Morven were missing, Dave looked through his notes on the case from the beginning.

It was his habit to keep a record of everything he discussed about a case, no matter how trivial it might seem at the time. He was amazed how many times this had come in useful in the past. One small detail, one snippet of conversation, could turn out to be the key that led to a major breakthrough in a case.

He often reviewed his notes just before the morning briefing. That way if something leapt out at him, he could run it by the rest of the team straight away.

He scanned the pages of his notebook, remembering some of the things he'd thought worth recording and being reminded of others that had slipped his mind. Although most of the 'paperwork' he did these days was computerised, for his own notes Dave favoured a good old-fashioned notebook and pen.

Aware that any records he made could potentially be used in evidence in court, he ensured he was always professional. He had to be able to swear that what he wrote was true. It wouldn't look good for a detective inspector to be sued by someone because of something defamatory he'd written about them.

Dave flicked through the notes that covered the day of Ayesha's abduction, not noticing anything he hadn't already considered a dozen times. The notes for Saturday covered the team briefing he'd given the day after the crime.

There it was — something that had been niggling at the back of his mind for days.

Morven had attended that briefing even though it was her day off. She had been fired up by the identification she thought she had made. Not of one of the two kidnappers themselves; she had tracked the CCTV back to the point where the pair had entered the airport terminal.

There had been a third man with them, but the camera only caught him as he turned and left the building. There were just a few seconds' worth of images and it only showed a partial image of the man's head. And yet Morven was convinced that man was John Whitehouse MP.

Dave had discounted this — reasonably, he thought. But in the absence of any other leads he decided to task someone with tracing the MP's movements at the time of the crime.

He'd already apologised to Morven

for ridiculing her theory. He only hoped he'd get a chance to tell her just how sorry he was for not pursuing the possible lead.

If it turned out that Whitehouse was involved, and if Morven ended up being harmed, Dave would never forgive himself.

* * *

Paula was ready to go. There was just one thing missing. She looked at her reflection in the full length mirror in Morven's bedroom. Her hair and make-up were perfect and the clothes she had borrowed fitted beautifully. Just one finishing touch and the plan would come together perfectly.

At that moment she heard the door buzzer. The delivery guy had arrived — and it was still only half past eight.

Hurrying back to the mirror once she had signed for the delivery, Paula was wearing her new contact lenses within moments. They didn't alter her vision but they were tinted dark brown.

It was amazing how much difference such a small thing made to her appearance. Combined with the dark brown hair dye, she had managed to transform herself so that she closely resembled Morven. She allowed herself a triumphant smile as she felt the final piece of the plan slot in.

Now Paula sat watching the minutes go by on the kitchen clock. Banks still stuck to a nine-to-five working day. At least, Morven's bank did.

Paula had gained access to Morven's bank accounts online weeks ago. She had installed spy software on Morven's computer that recorded all her key strokes and sent them to Paula's laptop. When Morven signed in to her online account Paula was able to find out her password and sign on herself later the same day. She had known Morven was rich, but the amounts she saw on there still surprised her.

The original plan had been to steal as much as possible by transferring money out online. Paula's partner in crime had set up several accounts at other banks using fake identities. They were frustrated by additional security checks by Morven's bank, which meant that the only way to access large amounts was for Morven to go in person and instruct her personal banker to make the transfers.

That was when the elaborate scheme to enable Paula to impersonate Morven was dreamed up.

At exactly nine o'clock Paula rang the bank and informed them she would be in at ten. As she'd predicted, this was acceptable. The old saying that money talks was obviously true.

Before she left the apartment, she checked that all her belongings were packed. Once her business at the bank was completed she would come back to collect her things and then . . . well, then it would be time to enjoy the rewards for the past few months of planning. She would have enough money to do whatever she wanted. And if anyone ever said that money couldn't buy happiness, then she'd tell them she'd rather be miserable and rich than miserable and poor.

As she walked towards the tube station Paula had a spring in her step. Just a few more hours and the miserable life she had been leading up to now would be over. She had so many dreams and ambitions that she could never have hoped to realise, but now they would all be possible.

The rush hour was over so she was able to find a seat on the train. Only a few stops and it would be time to get into character and become Morven.

There were just a few doubts at the back of her mind preventing her from enjoying this performance as much as she could have. Firstly she was worried that there might be someone at the bank, other than the absent personal banker, who knew Morven well and would notice something different when Paula walked in.

Second and possibly more likely, the

police might have informed the bank of Morven's disappearance. For all Paula knew, that might be standard practice when someone went missing. Maybe they put a stop on people's bank accounts or something. That would obviously be a disaster.

The third thing bothering Paula was something that had troubled her before, on occasion. It was something about her own personality that she would never have admitted to anyone. Paula had an unusual trait, one she had seen portrayed in films and on TV, and it worried her.

She did not feel a trace of guilt about what she was doing to Morven; she was one of those people who had been born without a conscience.

The reason it worried her was that whenever she saw people like her on TV, they were referred to as psychopaths.

10

Morven woke early from a fitful sleep. Thankfully Pete Harris had been sympathetic and had untied her from the uncomfortable chair. He'd even removed the harsh plastic ties from her wrists when she'd asked if she could use the bathroom. However once she'd returned to the long room, Harris had left and locked the door behind him.

Yasmeen and Ayesha, along with the travel cot, had been moved to another room and Morven had been left alone with just the sofa to sleep on.

It could have been worse, she thought. A sofa was better than the floor. Before she settled down for the night, she tried all the windows but they were locked.

Any thought of being able to break the glass was pointless. The windows were double-glazed and even if she could have smashed one, the noise would have alerted her captors.

Bright sunshine lit up the room now and Morven looked out to try and get an idea of her surroundings. As she looked down into the yard, a line of horses and riders was passing by.

The beautiful animals were all at the peak of fitness and condition and she realised she was watching a string of racehorses being taken out for a training session. It didn't take long to connect that thought to the Khalil family's links to horse racing.

And John Whitehouse's links too, she thought.

As if she had willed it by that thought, a man who was the spitting image of John Whitehouse emerged from a building on the other side of the yard. His brother, Morven realised.

Cogs were whirring in her brain, trying to make sense of all this, and to make it fit with what Yasmeen had told her last night.

Once she had started, Morven hadn't

been able to shut her up, so she had sat and listened, only asking a few questions, while Yasmeen got everything off her chest. Everything, that is, except the name of the man who was behind what had happened.

'You have to believe me,' she had said. 'We never meant for anyone to get hurt. That poor woman at the airport. She was so young and I was devastated when I heard that she had died. Our plan was just to make it look convincing that Ayesha had been kidnapped. Then a few days later I would disappear, too. Both of us would be gone without a trace. The police would stop looking for us eventually and by then we would be living our new lives.'

'So all this was just because you wanted to leave your husband?'

'It's hard for someone who lives here to understand. In Dubai I am hardly allowed out of our home on my own. Admitting to being in an unhappy marriage would be unthinkable. If I left or asked for a divorce, that would be seen as dishonouring my husband's family. They simply would not accept or allow it.

'I can see by your face that you think I'm exaggerating. But it's true. My sister-in-law, Hamid's brother's wife, tried to leave five years ago. She was a beautiful woman but when the family found her and brought her back she had terrible injuries to her face. Now she wears a scarf at all times to cover the scars.

'We have become close over the years since then and the things she has told me give me nightmares. I feel so guilty about leaving her behind with no hope of escape and now no friend to comfort her. But I know I had no choice — it was now or never.

'I knew that in the unlikely event I managed to get away from Hamid and his family, they certainly would not let me take our child with me. I would have nothing — no home, no money, I could not survive on my own. I needed help but over the years being under the constant surveillance of my husband I had lost touch with most of my old friends.'

'So what changed? Who came up with this plan?' Morven asked.

'One of the few places I'm allowed some freedom is at the races. In Dubai the trainers' wives are able to attend and socialise. It is a kind of competition to show off the beautiful clothes and jewellery my husband has provided for me. In this country I can mix with owners and trainers and their families. The rules are relaxed and although I still have to be careful not to do anything that might disgrace my husband's family, Hamid relaxes his hold on me for a while. It wouldn't do for his British racing friends to see his true character.

'So I can enjoy an almost normal time on those days. That is how I met my . . . friend. I first met him three years ago. We would see each other at various racecourses and as time went on, we would look forward to these meetings more and more. I didn't dare keep in touch at any other time. My husband monitors my phone and my computer use. But I have one trusted woman friend, the wife of another trainer, who agreed to pass messages between us.'

Yasmeen's eyes had misted over and she had a distracted look on her face.

Morven realised that Yasmeen was starting to enjoy her reminiscence. *Incredible*, she thought. *It's fine for her to get all sentimental about her love affair — she's not the one sitting here in fear for her life.*

Morven must have given away her annoyance at this by her body language and Yasmeen continued more seriously.

'After a while, just seeing each other at the races every so often and snatching a few minutes' conversation wasn't enough for either of us. We found, er, somewhere we could meet.' Yasmeen was becoming evasive now, obviously not wanting to spell out to Morven the exact details. 'We would arrange these meetings and if one of us had to cancel we would contact my friend who would pass the message on. She was also my alibi. In this country Hamid would allow me to visit a friend for a few hours without him. That arrangement carried on for a few months but then I found out I was pregnant and Hamid refused to allow me to travel from Dubai to England any longer.'

Yasmeen lowered her eyes. These memories were obviously not so pleasant.

Morven had to ask the obvious question.

'Is Ayesha your husband's child?'

Yasmeen looked her in the eye but refused to answer. It was a few moments before she continued her story.

'After Ayesha was born, Hamid became even more controlling. I've hardly left our home for the past year. Oh, he still let me out for the big events in the horse racing calendar. People would have started to ask questions otherwise.

'My friend came over to Dubai. We

hadn't seen each other for so long, and he was willing to travel all that way once I managed to pass a message to him that I would be at a high profile event that was coming up. He has connections to racing and it wouldn't seem odd for him to travel for that purpose.

'When I saw him, it was like falling in love all over again. The thought of going back to being a virtual prisoner in my home was unbearable. I knew I had to try and find a way to escape. That's how we ended up here.'

Last night Morven hadn't managed to fit the final piece of the jigsaw, but now she did. If this house was at the training yard of John Whitehouse's brother, it wasn't too much of a leap to guess that the MP was Yasmeen's 'friend' who had come up with the abduction plan.

For a moment, she felt a glow of satisfaction at having been right about John Whitehouse. After the humiliating talking-to she'd been given by Dave Bradley in front of the whole team, how satisfying it would have been to hear him having to admit she'd been right all along.

Then reality kicked in and she realised there was every chance she would never see Dave again — never mind hear him acknowledge such a thing.

Morven felt powerless in her current situation. At least when Yasmeen had been in this room with her she might have had a chance to talk her into convincing John Whitehouse to let her go. Now she had no way of talking to Yasmeen or anyone else.

She wished she had pressured Yasmeen into answering her last night when she had questioned Ayesha's paternity. If the child was not Hamid's then she could almost understand Yasmeen's desperation to escape him. If he ever found out that Ayesha was not his, and with his wealthy and powerful family behind him, who knew what would have become of Yasmeen and the child?

Morven's head was spinning with the frustration of being unable to do anything with the knowledge she had gained. Silently she willed her team mates, and especially Dave Bradley, to catch on to the connection with the MP.

If they didn't, then how on earth would she ever be rescued?

Morven had always prided herself on being resourceful and intelligent. But after hours of trying to come up with a way of escaping this situation, she had to admit it was no use. She was completely at the mercy of her captors. Their original plan had obviously never included abducting a police officer. The fact that their team included one former police officer and one who was still employed by the Met meant that they would be well aware of the penalty for doing so.

Added to the tragic death of Carly Simmonds, they were all facing lengthy prison sentences if they were caught. Yasmeen might be able to plead that she was trying to flee an abusive spouse but the others were all in it up to their necks — conspiracy, child abduction . . . the list of offences was growing.

Morven thought her best hope might be if they all decided to flee in an attempt to evade justice. But would they leave her behind, or would they decide that it was too dangerous to allow her to remain alive and able to identify them all?

The terrifying conclusion Morven was coming to was that they may well decide their only option was to silence her. Forever.

11

Dave Bradley was taking advantage of ten minutes' peace to sit back in his office chair and try to get his thoughts in order.

The team briefing had been more subdued than usual. The disappearance of one of their colleagues had made everyone even more determined to crack this case, but there was still a sense of frustration at their lack of progress.

What could they do in an abduction case where the kidnappers didn't get in touch with any demands? A few members of the team were still suspicious of Hamid Khalil, and Dave was careful to consider each of their comments. He'd learned a lesson about discounting what anyone said in the briefing.

'Are we sure he hasn't been contacted but told not to inform us?' one of them asked.

'We're monitoring the apartment and his mobile phone,' someone else piped up.

'Or maybe it's he who has harmed both his daughter and his wife. I know he wasn't in the country last Friday but he could have organised it,' said another.

Dave was still pretty sure Hamid Khalil wasn't involved. He didn't have to like the guy to give him the benefit of the doubt. In fact the longer time went on, the more sympathy Dave felt for Hamid.

However a sympathetic attitude was no use to him when he went from the briefing to his boss's office to update her. She wasn't nicknamed She Who Must Be Obeyed for nothing.

The Detective Chief Inspector managed the various teams she supervised with a no-nonsense attitude. If you did your job well and got results, everything was fine. If she suspected you were giving less than a hundred percent you were in big trouble.

Despite Dave's years of experience and his reputation as an exceptional police officer, he still felt slightly anxious whenever he had to admit to her that things weren't going well. He knew she had developed her strict management style because, ultimately, she was responsible for everything the teams under her did. Once he had updated her, she would have to answer to the next in line and so on up the ranks.

'Do I need to bring someone else in on this, Dave?' the DCI had asked him this morning.

Dave was taken aback. He had never been replaced on an investigation and he didn't want to start now. Yet a twinge of something that might have been guilt made him wonder whether she might be right to consider it.

Refusing to listen to the internal voice that was questioning his competence, Dave had assured his boss emphatically that he could cope.

'I'll give you another forty-eight hours,' she said. 'If we haven't wrapped up this case by then I'll have to reconsider.'

Now, Dave sat thinking back over that conversation. Forty-eight hours. Half as long as they'd already spent on this case with no results. Forty-eight hours with God knows what happening to the woman he loved. That thought brought him to his senses as it was the first time he'd admitted it, even to himself.

A light knock on the glass door of his office interrupted his brooding and one of his detective constables came in.

'I've got that information you wanted about John Whitehouse, boss. Sorry it wasn't ready in time for the briefing.'

'No problem — let's have a look at what you've got.'

Dave quickly scanned the few sheets of typed notes that the officer handed to him and his hope of linking Whitehouse to the abduction faded away. The MP had spent the whole of Friday morning at a hospice helping to raise funds at an event. He had taught his team well and they had been thorough in their research, visiting the hospice and questioning several people who confirmed they had spoken to John Whitehouse.

A note on the final page caught Dave's eye. The officer who had prepared the report had noted that the hospice manager had offered to provide CCTV footage if necessary.

'I hope you were discreet with your questions,' Dave said. 'I can do without being sued for defamation of character if the MP finds out we've been asking questions about him.'

'Don't worry,' the DC said. 'We didn't mention a specific enquiry and we kept our questions very general. Most of the people we spoke to offered John Whitehouse's name before we even asked about him. He's quite the local celebrity as well as their MP.'

'Good work,' Dave said. The note about the CCTV had stuck in his mind. It might be yet another dead end but what harm could it do?

'Can you ask Sergeant Foster to put one of her team onto following up this offer of CCTV?' Dave noticed a change in the DC's expression. 'I know they're short-staffed with PC Jennings missing. And I'm sure they're all worried about her — and maybe even more than the rest of the team.' As he said this Dave hoped that his own fears for Morven weren't reflected on his face. 'But I'm sure, too, that PC Jennings would want everyone to be putting all their effort into reuniting the Khalil family and bringing her back where she belongs.'

'OK, boss. And by the way we've tried to contact John Whitehouse this morning but he's unavailable.'

The DC turned on his heel and hurried off to find Sergeant Foster.

Odd that the MP had gone to ground after being all over the TV news for days, Dave thought. He felt happier once he'd set in motion organising the CCTV. He'd learned a long time ago never to ignore his instincts and there was something about the MP's alibi of the hospice event that was niggling at him. He knew he wouldn't relax until it was followed up.

There was something else about John Whitehouse that Morven had mentioned. Something that linked him to the Khalils, beyond the fact that he was the MP for the constituency where their London home was located.

Dave left his office and went over to Morven's desk. It had been searched thoroughly in case it held any clue to her disappearance, but everything had been put back in place when the search drew a blank. Morven's work space was always neat and tidy — there were no sticky notes cluttering the desk or computer screen.

In the top drawer was a notebook and Dave flicked through the most recently used pages. Morven had been scribbling notes about her research into John Whitehouse's background. And there it was. He had grown up living at a racehorse training stables that was now run by his brother.

Dave switched on the computer on Morven's desk and signed into the system. He did a few searches and found out where the Whitehouse business was. Then he searched for the Newmarket stable where Hamid Khalil's uncle had his horses trained.

Dave knew that Newmarket was dominated by the horse racing industry and that there were dozens of stables based there. But when he looked at a map it was clear that the two stables he was interested in were virtually next door to each other.

Dave decided to send two officers over to Newmarket this morning, making a quick call to the local police to keep them in the loop and let them know that assistance might be required later. Whether the MP had an alibi for last Friday or not, there were too many coincidences showing up now for him to ignore.

He only wished he had taken Morven seriously when she had suggested exactly that. He was feeling more positive now that there were new leads to follow up, but he still had a constant feeling of dread hanging over him.

What would he do if something terrible had happened to Morven and he hadn't been able to prevent it?

* * *

Paula was sitting in the comfortable waiting area at the bank. It definitely wasn't your usual high street bank branch. Instead of a glass-screened counter there were several partitioned seating areas where clients were greeted by smartly dressed staff.

Having been there a while, Paula had noticed refreshments being brought to some of the tables. She'd certainly never been offered a cup of tea when she'd been called in to her bank to explain why she was so far over her overdraft limit.

She was starting to get slightly worried about the delay. When they'd been planning this, the one thing they were certain of was that the bank staff would bend over backwards to keep Morven Jennings happy. Someone with the amount Morven had in her various accounts would be used to the highest standards of service. So how come she, or at least Paula's impersonation of her, had been sitting here for nearly half an hour?

People who'd arrived after her were already enjoying a cuppa and a chat in one of the meeting areas. For all her usual confidence and bravado Paula was now tapping her foot impatiently and would have appreciated the offer of a drink because her mouth was suddenly very dry.

For the second time in the last ten minutes a man dressed very smartly in a dark suit and red tie glanced over at her from the reception desk and then spoke quietly into his phone. Something felt wrong about this. Very wrong.

Moments later two uniformed police officers entered the bank and walked towards the reception desk. The dark suited man pointed over to the waiting area, then did a double-take. The place where Paula had been sitting was empty.

One of the police officers ran back to the main entrance and looked both ways down the street but there was no sign of anyone running away.

'She was there just one minute ago. I'd told her the member of staff she was waiting for was delayed, exactly as I was instructed.' The dark-suited man was finding it hard to believe that he hadn't noticed the woman disappear.

If there was one thing Paula prided herself on, it was her quick wits. When the feeling of something being wrong persisted, she had quickly made her move, slipping out of the main door at the same time as the police officers were going in.

She knew that if she ran she would make herself conspicuous, so she simply went into the coffee shop next door and sat at the table furthest from the window. While she waited for the waitress to take her order she removed the dark brown lenses from her eyes and tied her hair back into a severe ponytail. Within moments, most of the resemblance to Morven was gone.

Taking off her jacket and stuffing it under the table, she was confident that if anyone looked into the café, they wouldn't pick her out.

By the time her drink arrived, Paula's heart rate had returned to normal and she was trying to work out how her visit to the bank and her plan to access Morven's money had been foiled.

She was dreading the call that she would have to make soon, to someone who would be expecting to hear that the plan had worked. Instead Paula was going to have to admit that it had failed — and that any future attempt may be impossible now that the bank were, somehow, aware of the threat.

* * *

Morven glanced at her watch as boredom and fear started to take their toll on her mood. She wondered if the manager at her bank had received the email she sent the previous day. If so, then hopefully he had put in place the measures that Morven believed to be necessary.

She had managed to work out the connection between Paula Gill dyeing her hair and ordering brown contact lenses and the business card she had found in the sitting room. Depressing as it was, it seemed that her apparent new best friend was planning some sort of fraud involving Morven's bank accounts.

The appointment had been for later in the week but Morven had wanted to play it safe so she had fired off the email that stated if anyone, including herself, turned up at the bank to discuss her affairs then the police should be called. Adding that she would explain further when the bank opened, she had trusted that the manager would take notice.

Of course by the time the bank had opened, a couple of hours ago, she hadn't been in a position to contact the manager. Although it had given her something to think about other than her current predicament, Morven realised that as far as priorities went money was pretty low down the list at the moment.

* * *

Any concerns Paula had that the police officers might come into the coffee shop faded after about half an hour. She'd spent the time people watching, wishing she could swap places with any one of the people sat at the other tables. It never crossed her mind to wonder if they might have troubles of their own to worry about.

She finished her drink, paid and left the coffee shop, hurrying to the Tube station. She was frustrated and puzzled that the bank plan had gone disastrously wrong but she was practical enough to know that her priority now was to move on and disappear.

One thing she couldn't avoid, though, was making the call to tell her partner in crime what had happened. They'd spent so many hours over the past several months working on this scheme. Paula knew she would get the blame for its failure but she also knew she needed help.

She eventually plucked up the courage to make the call when she was walking back from the Tube to the apartment. All her things were packed and ready to go — but to go where? She was relying on the fact that the arrangements for fleeing the country were all in place. The only problem was that instead of now being rich, she was still broke and was now on the run from the police. What a difference a few hours made.

Paula felt better once she'd made the call. Her co-conspirator had been surprisingly understanding.

'We always knew there was a chance it wouldn't work.' There wasn't a hint of anger or disappointment in the voice. 'Go home and wait. I'll come over with some cash to tide you over until things calm down.'

Paula let herself into the apartment for what she knew would be the last time. No matter what had happened to Morven, she was hardly likely to look kindly on Paula if she suspected what she had tried to do. The bank or the police would inform her as soon as she was found. One look at the bank's CCTV would be all Morven needed to recognise Paula despite her disguise.

Pacing the kitchen floor, Paula began to realise just how crazy the impersonation plan had been. And it was she who had taken all the risks while the other person sat back and waited for a phone call! Paula vowed that she would come up with a plan to get her hands on a fortune without taking risks. And she would do it by herself next time.

The buzzer sounded and Paula pressed the button without bothering to look at the screen. She knew who it would be. Now all she wanted to do was get her hands on the cash she'd been promised and get out of here.

She opened the door, an eager expression on her face.

'Thanks for coming. I need to . . . '

Paula's voice faded away. Standing behind the person she was expecting were two female police officers.

'I'm sorry, Paula, there was nothing else I could do. Once I realised you'd tried to steal Morven's money I had to contact the police.' Jenny Mason, Morven's permanent witness protection liaison officer, stood back as the police officers entered the apartment to arrest Paula.

'But . . . Jenny, how could you? You said you'd help me — bring me some money.'

'I've no idea what she's talking about, officers,' Jenny said.

'We'll take it from here,' one of them answered. 'And our colleagues will be picking up Ben Gill. We'll be in touch if we need any more information.'

When the police officers had left with Paula, Jenny wandered around the apartment. She'd been here several times, of course, before her maternity leave. Now she felt as if she was looking at it through fresh eyes.

Her envy of Morven's wealth had started soon after she began working with the young woman. Jenny had worked her way up from a terrible start in life, determined to escape the poverty she was brought up in. She'd been satisfied with her good job in witness protection and her modest flat on the outskirts of London.

She remembered the day her supervisor handed Morven's case to her, even though she was a relatively new member of the team.

'I'm giving you this one because I think she'd benefit from being teamed up with one of our younger team members,' her supervisor had said. 'And I think you're ready for a complex case.'

'Complex?' Jenny had asked. 'In what way?' She was scanning the notes in the case file as she waited for an answer.

'Dreadful case. Both parents murdered; the girl was there. We've got her because she saw the killer and he hasn't been apprehended yet.'

Up to that point Jenny had only worked with people who had testified in court cases and were under threat of harm from the criminals they'd incriminated or their associates. An unsolved double murder was definitely the most unusual case Jenny had been involved in.

She hit it off with Morven from the first time they met, and for the first few years she found it rewarding and enjoyable to help Morven build herself a new life.

She couldn't put her finger on when things changed. Probably it was just an accumulation of events that chipped away at the friendship the two women had developed.

When Morven moved into this apartment Jenny had definitely started to feel bitter and envious. Morven was spending money like there was no tomorrow at a time when Jenny was starting to feel the pinch of the high rent on her flat and was tired out by the commute each day because she couldn't afford to live any closer to her central London office base at the National Crime Agency.

It became a pattern that when she had to meet with Morven she needed to force herself to put on a smile and work in Morven's best interests. She would go home on those days more exhausted that by any other cases she worked on. When she was faced with the prospect of becoming a single parent, something snapped and that was when the plan to steal Morven's money started to form in her head.

The idea had come to her when Ben Gill had asked her if she thought it would be appropriate for him to suggest his cousin as a flatmate for Morven. Ben had been appointed to cover Jenny's maternity leave and he was such a stickler for the rules, he had phoned her at home just after he took over the case.

'Do you think it would be OK, Jenny?' he'd asked. 'Paula's desperate for somewhere to stay and I think it'd do Morven good to have some company.'

Jenny knew the proposed set-up would never be approved in a million years. The risk of Morven's witness protection status being exposed was huge. But Ben had shared something about Paula that left her open to manipulation and Jenny immediately realised she could use it to her advantage.

'She's had a tough year,' he said. 'This guy she was working for started a relationship with her but forgot to mention he was married. When she found out she went off the rails — stalked his wife, did some damage to their house. She needs a complete change of scene and then I'm sure she'll be fine.'

Jenny had advised Ben to go ahead and suggest Paula as a flatmate, but to make sure there was no record of the family relationship with Ben in Morven's witness protection file. He would have to document the change to Morven's living arrangements but Jenny suggested he should alter Paula's surname so she couldn't be linked to him.

Jenny knew that by following her advice Ben was effectively setting himself up to be sacked, or worse, if anyone found out what he'd done. Falsifying details in a client's file was a serious matter.

Without Ben's knowledge Jenny contacted Paula and befriended her. Skilled at psychological manipulation, she convinced Paula that she was entitled to a share of Morven's wealth and over the weeks they developed their plan.

Now it had failed, Jenny's priority was to make sure she came out of this squeaky clean. She had made preparations for this outcome by altering Ben's computer files to point the finger of suspicion at him. Being a senior team member she was able to access the files from home. As things stood, there was every chance Ben would take the fall for Jenny's crimes. And Paula couldn't implicate Jenny without first admitting that she herself was guilty.

Jenny's brain was overflowing with all the things that had happened that morning and only now did she start to wonder where Morven was. Seconds later, she started to work out the possibilities for getting her hands on some of Morven's money if she never came back.

There were several expensive art works in the apartment. In the early days Morven had wanted to retrieve some of her mother's paintings from the old house but Jenny had to explain to her that everything from her old life had been sold. As a symbolic tribute to her mother, who had loved art, Morven had begun a small collection of exquisite paintings.

There was also a large box of jewellery in Morven's bedroom — she had been recreating her mother's belongings in that area too.

Jenny emptied the box into her bag. If Morven did return, everyone would think Paula had stolen it. If she didn't, then maybe Jenny would make another trip back for the paintings.

For now she had to get home. Her

sister was babysitting and she'd already texted twice to ask when Jenny would be back. It was time to find a proper childminder.

If she kept her head and carried on life as normal, Jenny reckoned she could get away with this whole thing. She smiled. If her plan to frame Ben worked, she might even be able to go back to her job early.

* * *

Morven was sure Pete Harris was close to cracking. Whatever hold Matt Hanlon had over him, he seemed to be questioning whether it was worth throwing away the rest of his life.

Morven didn't even know the full details of why the pair had been kicked off the team. Of course there had been the usual station gossip but there were so many theories, there was no way of knowing the truth. Dave Bradley was far too professional to have given any clues.

Morven felt butterflies in her stomach at the thought of Dave but she told herself to get a grip. It was time to give Pete Harris a nudge towards what she was sure he wanted anyway.

'Pete, have you thought about what will happen when this is all over?' she asked, the next time Pete arrived with a drink and some food for her.

At first she thought he was going to ignore her but then he gave his usual scared glance over his shoulder to make sure nobody could hear.

'We'll be long gone before anyone figures out what's happened,' he said.

'You're not stupid enough to believe that,' Morven said. She was on dodgy ground now. Pete had been kind to her so far. Was it really a good idea to risk changing his attitude to her?

Yet what was the alternative? Just sit there and wait to see what happened? No, Morven would always rather do something than nothing.

'What is it, Pete? What's the hold that Hanlon has over you?'

Pete sat next to her with a deep sigh, rubbing his eyes with the heels of his hands. He looked weary, as if he hadn't slept in days.

'He stole evidence,' Pete said, as if that explained everything.

Morven knew that if she waited long enough Pete would continue. She was right.

'That case that collapsed last month. Dismissed due to insufficient evidence. It was because Matt owed someone a favour and he stole some key evidence from the evidence store and got rid of it. I'm surprised it didn't hit the headlines because the prosecution lawyers were livid.' He clammed up now as if he shouldn't even have said this much.

'OK,' Morven said. 'That explains why Hanlon was fired. What about you?'

'I knew he'd done it and I kept quiet. We go way back. There's things he's done for me that I can never repay. Although they suspected I was involved in the stolen evidence, they couldn't prove it. That's why I was just demoted and not fired. I'm still on the force, even if it's in uniform.

'So when he left and started work for the security company, he gave me a call. Reminded me of everything I owe him and said I could be their man on the inside if ever they needed it.'

'Pete, you know you should've reported it. Up till then all you would've lost was your job. Now you're in so deep Hanlon's going to drag you down with him.' The look on Pete's face told her he'd already realised this. 'But you could still do some good — maybe get a more lenient sentence. You just need to end this now. Contact DI Bradley and tell him where we are, and then — '

Morven didn't manage to finish her sentence. Matt Hanlon pushed the door fully open and entered the room, clapping his hands slowly.

'Oh, good effort, PC Jennings. You've got him eating out of the palm of your hand. But I'm afraid your buddy Pete's got a job to do.' He jerked his head towards the door and Harris scurried away. 'I think our Pete's a little sweet on you, Morven. But he's a bit busy right now so just leave him alone, OK? I heard your pathetic attempt at psychological persuasion but it won't work. We have our exit plan and we're about to use it.'

Hanlon left, locking the door behind him. Morven ran to the door, rattling it and hammering on it with her hands even though she knew it was useless.

For a few moments she'd thought she was having an influence on Pete Harris. That she was doing something to make a difference to her situation. Now she had to admit she was back to waiting frustratedly for someone else to act.

Eventually she walked slowly back to the sofa and sat down, defeated. Hanlon had mentioned an exit plan, and Morven didn't dare imagine what it might involve. His attitude to Morven ever since she'd been their prisoner gave her the impression he wouldn't think twice about harming her if he thought it would help them get away with what they'd done.

Although Morven was usually down to earth, her imagination was in danger of running away with her now. And the images it was creating in her head were so frightening, she could feel the veneer of bravery she had been trying to maintain since she got here cracking.

Just as she was about to give in to tears she heard a loud bang. It was a noise that transported her back ten years in time — the unmistakable sound of a gunshot.

12

When the two officers Dave had sent to Newmarket reported back about their visit to Mark Whitehouse's training stables, they'd both been in agreement. There was something odd about the trainer's manner that they couldn't put their finger on.

For someone who was a famous figure in his sport, he had come across as very nervous and evasive. One of the officers remembered seeing him interviewed on TV once and he'd come across as a very confident individual.

'We're making routine enquiries at several premises in Newmarket, sir.' One of the officers had taken the lead. 'It's connected to the abduction of Ayesha Khalil, her mother and one of our officers.'

Mark Whitehouse obviously realised a response was expected. He pulled himself together and tried to think what a normal reply would be.

'How can I help?' was the best he could come up with.

'Are you able to assure us there is nowhere on your property where those people could be?'

'Absolutely. I check every inch of this place morning and night,' Mark said. 'There's no way anyone could be hidden here without my knowledge.'

It was only later when they were comparing notes that they examined Mark's comments more closely. There was no way anyone could be hidden there without his knowledge, but what about *with* his knowledge? At the other premises they'd visited they had been invited to look around throughout the house, stables and outbuildings. But at the Whitehouse stables they had basically been fobbed off.

The two officers decided to visit the local police headquarters and that's when they contacted Dave Bradley.

'What do you think, boss? Should we go back?'

'No, stay where you are for now,' Dave said. 'I'll liaise with the locals and you can go back with them later.'

It took a while to co-ordinate a search team to visit the Whitehouse stables. Dave had just put the phone down for the final time, planning to wait in his office for the search team to report back, when his mobile rang.

'Boss, they're going to have to put the search on hold,' an agitated voice told him. 'There's reports of shots fired at the Whitehouse stables. The guy in charge here is calling in the armed response team.'

* * *

The armed response team was stationed at the county's police headquarters. When the call came through that a firearm was involved in a suspected kidnapping, the team was sent to the Whitehouse stables immediately.

Meanwhile Matt Hanlon had burst into the room where Morven was being held.

'Time for you to be of some use,' he said to her as he locked the door behind him and barricaded it with a heavy table.

'What's going on?' Morven asked. The gunshot had terrified her, throwing her back in time to those terrible memories of ten years earlier. In her confusion she looked at Hanlon now and wondered if he had come here to assault her. When she saw the gun in his hand, she began to tremble with fear.

'Pete's lost it,' Hanlon said, shaking his head. 'I didn't even know he had a gun with him. I knew he was struggling, but not like this. He ran away from me and by the time I caught up with him he'd tried to top himself.'

'You left him after he'd shot himself?' Morven was horrified.

'The idiot missed,' Hanlon said. 'Barely grazed his ear. Now he's sat there muttering to himself about not even being able to do that. I grabbed the gun from him and came back here.'

'Where are the others?' Morven

asked. She was relieved nobody had been seriously injured, or worse, by the shot she'd heard. She hadn't realised how badly it would affect her to hear a gunshot again.

Fortunately she was unlikely to come into contact with anyone who used guns in her day-today life, but if and when she ever got out of here she would have to think seriously about seeing a counsellor to talk about the issue. The sessions of counselling she'd had in the early days after her parents' deaths had concentrated more on the bereavement rather than the manner of their deaths. Now Morven knew the legacy of that night could cause her to suffer flashbacks whenever she heard a gun fired.

'They're all huddled together in the kitchen. I tried to leave the stables but a police van was already heading up the drive.' Hanlon was agitated and struggling to think straight. He couldn't believe how soon his clever exit plan had come to nothing.

'You know there's no way out of this,' Morven said as calmly as she could. 'If they're aware of the gun there'll be armed officers out there.'

'But I've got you, haven't I?'

Morven's heart sank as she realised Hanlon had stopped thinking rationally altogether. He seemed to think he was in the middle of an action movie. Once again, she was afraid her life was really in danger. In a locked room with a desperate man who had a loaded gun.

Morven took several deep breaths to try and regulate her breathing. It was time to try and talk some sense into Hanlon. It was also time to delve back into her memory, to her police training. They'd been given a basic understanding of how to deal with someone who was in crisis.

Matt Hanlon was displaying all the signs of a person on the verge of losing touch with reality. Morven needed to use her skills to cool the situation down. The first thing she needed to do was calm herself down so she could then start to work on Hanlon.

A key factor in determining whether she would have any chance of success was whether she could convince Hanlon that he had a future if he gave himself up.

That was a big ask — Hanlon wasn't stupid. He'd also been in the police force long enough to know exactly what he was up against here.

Fortunately for Morven she was naturally skilled at being an active listener and being able to see the other person's point of view in any situation. Her awareness of this made her slightly more optimistic.

'Think of your family, Matt,' she said softly. 'OK, you might be facing some time in prison — but you'll be out and back with them in a couple of years' time.'

This was all guesswork — Morven had no idea what penalties Hanlon was facing.

'Family?' Hanlon's expression turned grim. 'That'd be my loving wife who left me and took the kids the day I was sacked from the force.'

This wasn't going well. At this rate Morven was going to escalate Hanlon's unstable mood. She racked her brain to try and come up with something to calm him down. She couldn't think of anything, and made a mental note not to bother applying for any hostage negotiator vacancies after all. So much for thinking she'd be good at this.

Movement through the window caught Hanlon's eye and he tugged Morven's arm to take her with him while he looked outside.

Yasmeen Khalil, clutching her daughter to her, was being hurried across the courtyard to a waiting police car.

Of course, thought Morven, *they have no idea that Yasmeen's involved.*

John and Mark Whitehouse were next, each led by a uniformed officer. Morven did a quick count up in her head, working out that the building was now empty apart from this room. Unless there were other people around that she didn't know about. But Hanlon confirmed her thoughts.

'Just us left,' he said grimly. 'In case you haven't worked it out yet, Sherlock, I've got nothing to lose. Might as well make yourself comfortable because I don't plan to make this easy for them.'

Morven moved towards the sofa on wobbly legs. She and Hanlon both knew that an armed response team would have arrived by now. It was standard procedure in a hostage situation where there was known to be a firearm involved. She didn't know what the tactics of the armed response team would be, but she didn't expect to get out of here any time soon.

* * *

Dave Bradley sat at his desk drumming his fingers and trying to stop himself running outside to his car and driving to Newmarket. He'd never felt so powerless in all his life. He glanced at his mobile phone and noticed two missed calls from Anne. He debated ignoring them but he knew she wouldn't try to contact him while he was working unless it was important.

She answered on the first ring.

'Oh, thank God you've called back,' she said, her voice sounding weary. 'The emergency's over now but I still wanted to let you know.'

She filled Dave in on what had been happening over the past couple of hours.

'I feel awful for not being there to help,' he said.

'Don't worry — I know you've got your hands full. But that situation they've been following on the news — that's Newmarket, right? So it's nothing to do with you.'

Actually it is my case,' Dave said. 'The locals are handling the hostage situation but I'm thinking of going over.'

Instantly her voice changed.

'Dave — for once in your life keep out of it. You said yourself they're handling it. And it could be dangerous.'

Dave ran a hand over his face.

'Anne, I know you worry about me but I can take care of myself. And I promise to stay away from the guys with the guns.'

Before they hung up Anne repeated what she said every time she spoke to him or saw him.

'I love you, Dave.'

'I love you too.'

Now Dave had made up his mind to go, he wanted to get on the road as soon as possible. He had faith in the armed response team's ability to bring the hostage situation to a peaceful conclusion, but something was telling him he needed to be there. He knew he couldn't be the one to rescue Morven — but at least he could be there to comfort her afterwards.

As he drove, Dave thought back to other cases he'd been involved with over the years. There had been times, of course, when he and his team had been unable to rescue victims of crime. Yet their successes were what made this job worthwhile.

He wouldn't allow himself to dwell on the possibility that Morven could end up being one of the unlucky ones. He had to stay positive and focused. He'd be no use to Morven if he turned up in an emotional state.

However one thing this case was teaching Dave was that he had to stop suppressing how he felt about Morven. To distract himself from his fears he started to try and work out a realistic plan for the future. A way forward where he and Morven could be together. The usual little nagging voice tried to tell him that Morven might not be interested — but from now on he was going to ignore that annoying voice.

* * *

Anne sat looking at her phone for a long time after she and Dave had disconnected the call. She was exhausted after an awful day and it would've been nice to have talked for a while longer. Or if Dave had offered to come over later.

But with Dave, the job always came first. When he was in the middle of a big case, he was distracted from everything else in his life.

Anne did her best to help — doing the stuff he tended to forget about, like laundry and making sure he remembered to eat something other than takeaways. She was always there to offer lifts home when he was too tired to drive, or when he'd had a few drinks on a night out with his team.

But when she needed some support, there always seemed to be something more important to keep him away. She knew there was no point trying to change Dave. He'd always been this way and he always would be. He'd been one of the most important people in Anne's life and she knew she was lucky to have him.

* * *

Dave's satnav told him he was within half a mile of his destination. He'd already passed several imposing entrances to long driveways that led to racing stables. The area was certainly dominated by them. Up ahead he could see the swirling blue lights of two police cars blocking the road. He parked up just this side of them and pushed his way through a crowd of press reporters. Further back down the road were three outside broadcast TV vans. These days, the TV news crews seemed to get to a crime scene faster than the police.

Dave introduced himself to one of the uniformed officers who were keeping the press and other onlookers back from the entrance to the Whitehouse stables, and asked him to point out the senior officer on the scene. Although the abduction of Ayesha Khalil was Dave's case, it was protocol and common courtesy to work in partnership with the local force.

Five minutes later Dave had been brought up to date on the situation. Yasmeen and Ayesha Khalil had been taken to the local headquarters where they would be accompanied by a family liaison officer. The child appeared to be unharmed and to have been well looked after. Hamid Khalil was on his way to be reunited with his wife and daughter.

Mark Whitehouse and his brother, John, had been arrested on suspicion of Ayesha's abduction and were in custody awaiting transfer to London. One unidentified male was under arrest but in hospital with minor injuries from a gunshot wound. A final unidentified male was holding a female hostage, believed to be PC Morven Jennings. The hostage taker was armed with a gun, believed to be the weapon that had injured the other suspect.

Dave took all this in and considered it for a few seconds. On the positive side, Ayesha and Yasmeen were safe and about to be reunited with Hamid. However Dave was unable to feel much satisfaction because overshadowing everything was the predicament that Morven was in.

All the way here, he'd been convincing himself that she'd be fine. That they would fall into each other's arms and he would keep her safe forever. Now the terrifying reality of the situation hit him and there was absolutely nothing he could do.

* * *

Morven couldn't bear to sit passively and wait for something to happen any longer. Her first attempt to talk some sense into Matt Hanlon had failed miserably, but she had been watching him every moment since then and she thought she'd detected a change in his mood.

'Matt, can we at least talk while we're stuck here with nothing else to do?'

He just shrugged. One more try, she decided.

'You probably think you've nothing to lose, like you said earlier. But look ahead a few years. There's no reason you couldn't try and make a fresh start.'

Matt turned a world-weary look on Morven.

'People like you can't understand what it's like to be so far down that it's impossible to see your way back up.'

'What do you mean, people like me?' Morven asked.

'Your life's so simple. So black and white. You've never made such a huge mistake that your whole life's ruined.'

Morven was angry now. How dare Matt Hanlon make assumptions about her life? For the first time since she'd entered witness protection she was tempted to tell her story. Then let Hanlon try and claim he'd had things harder than her.

The ingrained training provided by Jenny and the National Crime Agency kicked in and kept her quiet. Instead she asked him about Ayesha's abduction.

'I know it wasn't you and Pete Harris that snatched the baby from Heathrow. So come on, tell me how it was done.'

Hanlon looked at her with a half smile, half sneer on his face.

'Whitehouse found me through the

security firm I'd just signed with. He wanted someone who could organise the kidnap, follow it up with grabbing the mother, then keep them both out of sight until the father was satisfied they'd gone forever. He's some kind of control freak apparently — no way the mother could end up with the kid just by leaving him.'

Morven nodded, encouraged that she had managed to get Hanlon to speak so freely. Now she was sure that the key to engaging him further was by keeping quiet and letting him spill out all the details. He almost seemed proud of what he'd done. 'Go on,' she said.

'I told him we needed someone on the inside and I put pressure on Pete. His job was meant to be keeping me informed of details of the investigation while the force were looking for the kid. Obviously that didn't quite work out, but that's what you get when you work with idiots like him.' Hanlon shook his head as if he couldn't believe he'd been stupid enough to enlist someone as unstable as Pete Harris.

'The next thing was, I knew me and Pete couldn't be the ones to actually take the baby from the check-in hall. There's so many CCTV cameras in that place I knew whoever did it would be captured from every angle. And after working with you and your lot for months I knew about your success rate at identifying people. Would've been too easy for you to pick out people you already knew. So I bunged a couple of ex-cons some cash just to go in with the flash bang, come out with the child and then disappear.'

'Why was John Whitehouse there? I never would have linked him to all this if I hadn't seen him on the CCTV for a few seconds, just at the entrance to the terminal.'

'Another damned control freak,' Hanlon said. 'He was meant to be waiting in a car in the short stay car park. My two men were supposed to swap the kid into his car and he would've been away while everyone else was trying to work out what had happened as the smoke cleared. I still don't know why he came up to the entrance. Anyway, it wasn't long before we had other things to worry about. You, for instance — getting in the way of the next part of our plan.'

'And what about the young woman who was killed? Don't you have a conscience about that?'

Morven could have bitten her tongue — she was meant to be engaging Hanlon, not antagonising him. But Hanlon seemed to be considering her question, though he was obviously relaxing as he looked at her with a half smile on his face, rather than any guilt or remorse.

Perhaps she wasn't so bad at this after all. She hoped her expression was encouraging as she willed him to open up to her. If he did she was sure she could eventually persuade him to give himself up. But just as Hanlon took a breath to speak, all hell broke loose.

The door burst open and two men dressed head to toe in black, carrying large guns, ran in, shoving the heavy table out of the way as if it weighed nothing. Matt Hanlon spun round but wasn't quick enough to react before a third man had him pinned to the floor, the gun Hanlon had been holding spinning out of his hand and landing near the window.

Shock and fear left Morven sitting frozen in place on the sofa looking between the three armed men. For the first time she could remember, the features of their faces didn't register with her but alarm bells were ringing in her brain. So much was happening at once that she couldn't make sense of what her instincts were trying to tell her.

Then a female officer came in.

'PC Jennings? Everything's OK now. Come along with me and we'll get you out of here.'

Morven followed her mutely. Relief flooded through her and the after-effects of such an adrenaline-fuelled one-to-one with Hanlon made her light-headed. She just hoped she wouldn't make a fool of herself by passing out.

She stumbled through the front door, hanging on to the officer's arm to stop herself falling. There was an ambulance in the courtyard and a paramedic came over to meet Morven.

'Come this way, please,' he said. 'We need to get you to hospital and have you checked over.'

'I'm fine,' Morven protested. 'Just a bit wobbly, that's all. Can't you check me out here?'

The paramedic didn't get a chance to answer before a tall man in a suit strode up and wrapped Morven in a bear hug.

'Oh, thank God you're OK,' he said, still holding her tight.

'Boss?' Morven squealed. She was torn between enjoying the warm, protective hug from Dave Bradley's strong arms and worrying what everyone who was watching would think.

Finally Dave relaxed his hold on her. He looked into her eyes and asked, 'You're sure you're not injured?'

'I'm f-f-fine, physically,' she stammered. 'Just feeling a bit overwhelmed.'

'Is there anything I can get for you?' Dave said.

This wasn't exactly the romantic reunion he'd imagined.

'What I really want is to go home,' she said.

The paramedic led her to the ambulance and she sat inside while he quickly examined her. Satisfied with her blood pressure and other vital signs, the paramedic seemed almost disappointed to have to agree with Morven.

'If you're sure you want to go I can't see any reason to stop you.'

He spent a couple of minutes tapping information into the onboard computer system and called for authorisation from his supervisor. He didn't like letting anyone who might be injured leave without a trip to hospital but he couldn't force her. There were plenty of people who needed and wanted their help out there.

Finally he let Morven know it was OK for her to leave and she stepped down from the ambulance back into

Dave Bradley's arms.

'Right, you can come back in my car,' Dave said. 'I just need to make a quick phone call to the local headquarters and make sure everything's under control with having the Whitehouse brothers and our two ex-colleagues transferred back to our station. Then we'll be off.'

At last Morven's brain started to work normally again.

'What about Yasmeen Khalil?' she asked.

'What about her? She'll have to make a statement about her abduction at some point but it's not a priority.'

'But . . . oh, of course you don't know.'

Morven was about to make the rest of Dave's night a whole lot more complicated.

* * *

When Hamid Khalil received the call to tell him his wife and daughter were safe and well and were waiting to be picked up at the police headquarters near

Newmarket, he had almost collapsed with relief. However that feeling only lasted a few seconds. If his wife was hoping for a tearful reunion and a return to their normal lives, then she was going to be sadly disappointed.

Since the Detective Inspector had left him earlier, he had spent the time doing a bit of detective work of his own. First he had contacted his uncle in Dubai and asked him for a favour. Next he had pored over his laptop screen for hours, going through the calendar and notes he had made about his wife's trips to England over the past few years.

Hamid had many friends and contacts in the horse racing community. He was well known in Dubai and had many successes to his name internationally, too. He had access to several sources of information regarding gossip about trainers' families.

It only took him a short time to find someone who was willing to be honest with him about Yasmeen. Hamid had sat brooding about what to do with this information and when the phone call came, it seemed to him to be a sign.

Before he set off for Newmarket, he checked on his phone map to make sure he knew where his uncle's trainer's stable was located. If he was planning to stay the night in Newmarket, that would be as good a place as any to use.

A loving, protective husband and father wouldn't want to make his wife and daughter endure a car journey after what they'd been through, now would he?

* * *

Dave Bradley was feeling guilty for delaying Morven's return home, but he couldn't ignore the information she had just given him. A quick detour to the local police headquarters wouldn't do too much harm, he decided. He left Morven in the car while he hurried into the station and quickly introduced himself to the desk sergeant.

'I need you to keep Yasmeen Khalil

here while I organise transport for her to London,' he said. 'It's just routine questioning at this stage but I want to make sure she isn't allowed to leave.'

The sergeant checked his computer screen and gave Dave an apologetic look.

'Too late, sir, I'm afraid. Mrs Khalil and her daughter were collected by her husband just a few minutes ago.'

Dave cursed silently. There was no use getting angry with the station staff — they'd had no reason to detain Yasmeen Khalil. She was hardly the number one priority in the investigation, after all. Yet if she was involved, as Morven had just told him, then she couldn't be allowed to escape justice. The family liaison officer who had briefly been looking after Yasmeen and Ayesha had come into the outer office and asked the sergeant what the problem was. Luckily he had some information that might help.

'Mr Khalil mentioned they were going to stay the night in Newmarket because he didn't want to tire his wife and daughter any further. He didn't say exactly where, but there was something about his uncle's stables — don't know if that helps?'

The officer hurried back to carry on with his usual duties.

Dave remembered that Khalil's uncle's horses were trained close to the White-house stables. He arranged for a couple of patrol cars to meet him there in ten minutes and hurried back to his car to explain to Morven what was happening. She was pale with fatigue but was keen to stay with Dave while he pursued the Khalils.

A few minutes later they were arriving at the stables, whose name Morven had remembered from her research on Monday.

The whole place was in darkness, a row of horseboxes and several four-wheel-drive vehicles parked neatly in the courtyard. It took a while to rouse anyone, but eventually a man appeared, yawning and tying his dressing gown as he greeted them at the front door.

Dave explained quickly why they were there and the man acknowledged his link to the Khalil family.

'But I haven't seen Hamid for some time,' he said. 'As fellow trainers we sometimes bump into each other at the races, but I hardly know him. It's his uncle I work for. I'm surprised he's told the police he's staying here. I certainly haven't heard from him.'

Puzzled, Dave asked the uniformed officers to search the premises on the unlikely chance that the Khalil family might be hiding somewhere, but when he thought about it, he realised the trainer who owned the place had already convinced him their search would be useless.

It dawned on Dave that Hamid Khalil had fooled him in order to get a head start back to London. Apologising to the patrol car officers for wasting their time, he got back in the car and set off. He calculated that Hamid Khalil had between half an hour and an hour's head start and Dave wasn't about to initiate a car chase.

He used the car's hands free phone to report these latest developments to the team back in London and told them to await his instructions. He was about half an hour into the drive when he realised something he should have thought of earlier. The uncle's private jet. That's where Hamid would be heading. But which airport?

He was back on the phone again, delegating the task of locating the jet to one of his detective constables. He knew he needed to concentrate on driving and getting Morven home safely.

* * *

When Dave Bradley pulled the car up outside Morven's apartment block he glanced over at her in the passenger seat and saw that she was fast asleep. He hated to wake her but he wanted to get her inside and settled back into her home as soon as possible. The list of things he needed to do was growing by the minute and although he'd had no rest, he knew he had to keep going to tie up this case once and for all.

'Morven,' he said, gently shaking her shoulder.

'Hmm . . . what is it?' she said as she surfaced from the much-needed sleep.

'We're home,' Dave said, only realising after he'd said it that it sounded as if he lived there too. Wishful thinking. He had decided on the drive back to give Morven a few days to get used to the idea of possibly being in a relationship with him.

'We're back,' he corrected himself, though she didn't seem to have noticed anything wrong.

Morven stretched and then took off her seatbelt. As they headed to the main door Morven was reminded how useful it was that her building didn't need a key to access it, just a code. Between leaving home on Monday and now, she'd managed to lose all the belongings she'd had with her. She couldn't wait to get inside and have a shower and a change of clothes. Once Dave had gone, of course.

He was being a bit distant with her now but she remembered the hugs and his concern over the past few hours, so she was letting herself hope that her feelings might be reciprocated after all.

Dave went into the apartment with her but refused the offer of a drink. He was satisfied that Morven would be safe — the security arrangements at this block were second to none.

'I need to go in to the station for a few hours,' he said. 'Maybe we could meet for dinner tomorrow or . . . '

'Or you could come here — I'll cook.' Morven didn't feel up to socialising but the idea of an intimate dinner with Dave was something she could definitely look forward to.

'Great. I'll ring you later,' Dave said. 'I'm not checking up on you, it's just . . . OK, I am checking up on you.'

Morven laughed. It felt good to have someone care about her and want to check she was alright. There was an awkward moment as Dave stood by the apartment door, apparently wondering what to do. Then he leaned forward and kissed Morven on the cheek before quickly leaving without another word.

Morven showered and changed into a tracksuit. All of a sudden she was wide awake and her thoughts were racing. She knew she wouldn't be able to sleep and she'd never been a fan of watching TV for watching's sake. Although she knew Dave would probably order her straight home again, Morven decided to call a taxi and go in to work.

Before jumping into the shower she had found her old spare mobile phone and plugged it in to charge. Within a few moments she received a text telling her the taxi was waiting outside.

On the way to the station Morven went over all the things that had happened since the so-called kidnapping last Friday. It made her head spin to think about everything, not just with the case but with her home life too.

She made a mental note to check her online bank account when she reached the office, to see if there were any messages about someone trying to access her accounts. There had been no sign of Paula at the apartment, although all her belongings were packed up as if she was planning to leave.

There was something else bothering her — something lurking just beyond reach in her memory. It was connected to what had happened when Matt Hanlon was being arrested. It just wouldn't come to her and she was becoming more and more frustrated.

For now, she just wanted to get back to work and back to as close to normal as she could.

As she opened the taxi door to get out she glanced across the road and saw someone she recognised. It was the blonde woman who had picked Dave up after that night out a few months ago, and who Morven had seen giving him a lift after work a few times since. She was taking what looked like a pile of dry cleaning out of the boot of her car. Then she locked the car and hurried towards the station entrance.

'Sorry about this,' Morven said to the taxi driver. 'But can you just take me straight back where we came from?'

No matter how wide awake or keen to work she was, there was no way Morven wanted to confront Dave Bradley and his girlfriend right now. How dare he make a date for dinner with her when he was obviously still seeing this other woman?

Or was it not a date at all? Just concern for a work colleague? It was so confusing. She sent Dave an abrupt text cancelling their arrangements for the following night, but giving no explanation.

Morven gave the driver an overly generous tip and watched as he drove away. She was feeling very agitated now and she knew that if she went back up to the apartment she would just be pacing the floor.

After a couple of days cooped up in

cars or one room at the stables, what she really wanted to do was run. It might not be the most sensible time to be doing it but she decided a quick jog beside the river was exactly what she needed.

She shoved her phone into her tracksuit pocket and set off. When she jogged in the morning she enjoyed listening to music on headphones but that wouldn't be a wise choice in the dark — she needed all her senses on alert. This might be a nice upmarket area, but that fact itself attracted its share of undesirables.

Twenty minutes, she promised herself, then she'd turn back. But the run did exactly what she'd wanted, undoing the stress and strain in her muscles and letting her breathe freely again. By the time she arrived back, panting and sweaty and in need of a shower again, at least an hour had passed.

Morven had just entered the first gate into the apartment complex when she heard running footsteps behind her.

She turned round just in time to hear a man swear as he realised the gate she'd gone through was about to lock behind her. In the next couple of seconds she registered his face and his black clothing and something clicked in her brain. Frozen in place, she watched as he slipped through the gate just before it closed. As he moved closer, she reached into her pocket for the item she always kept there. She wouldn't have felt safe running in the city without it.

As the man reached his arms out towards Morven's neck she lifted her own hand and sprayed him full in the face at point-blank range with pepper spray.

His howl of pain shocked her into movement at last and before he could attempt to clear his eyes, she had turned on her heel and sprinted to the door of the building, pressing the entry code in record time. A burst of recognition had hit her just before she sprayed the man's face.

One thought was now going round

and round in her head — *that's the man who killed my parents*.

On the way up in the lift she dialled Ben's number but it was unavailable. Who could help her? She rejected the idea of calling Dave Bradley — he was too busy and it was all just too complicated. The next person she tried, the call went straight to voicemail and Morven left a brief message asking them to come round if possible. Then she had an idea, and dialled the one person she'd been able to rely on for years.

* * *

Morven tried to stay calm, sitting in the kitchen waiting for someone to respond to her call for help. *My parents' killer is a cop?* That was the question that kept shouting in her brain.

Well, he was a member of an armed police unit now and she had seen him twice tonight. But had he been a police officer back then?

If that was true, then she was amazed she had survived so long in witness protection. She knew the National Crime Agency's security was good but it wasn't infallible. Someone so close to being on the inside would have an advantage if they were trying to find a witness and silence them.

And this man, the one she was now certain she had recognised from ten years ago, was lurking nearby. Morven didn't know how long the pepper spray would put him out of action.

She didn't have to sit worrying for long because in next to no time the buzzer sounded and Morven saw Jenny Mason standing there.

How had she got there so quickly? Morven didn't care — she was just glad that Jenny had apparently dropped everything and found someone to look after her baby so quickly.

She pressed the button to allow Jenny into the building then waited with her hand on the front door handle until she heard the lift arrive. All the emotion and stress of the last few days seemed to erupt and Morven fell into Jenny's arms, sobbing. Jenny made comforting noises and stroked Morven's hair until the sobs started to subside.

'Hey, come on,' she said eventually. 'You're OK now, I'm here.' She led Morven by the hand into the sitting room, settling her on one of the large sofas. 'I'll make us both a drink and you can tell me all about it.'

'Did you report what I told you on the phone?' Morven asked, hiccupping as she tried to calm down from her crying fit. How could Jenny have got here so quickly if she'd spent anytime putting in a report to the National Crime Agency?

'It's all under control,' Jenny said. 'Technology's so wonderful these days — I did it on my phone in the taxi on my way here.'

Morven sat back and tried to relax but something still didn't feel right. Jenny went into the kitchen, returning a few minutes later with two steaming mugs of creamy hot chocolate.

'I thought this would be better than coffee,' she said. 'We need to calm you down a bit so you can get some rest. Now tell me again, slowly, what happened.'

Morven sighed. 'I went for a run and when I came back a man followed me through the entrance gate. I was still yards away when I looked at his face and it triggered a memory. Well, two memories. First, I recognised him as one of the armed response team at Newmarket and I realised why I'd felt so weird at that moment when they ended the hostage situation. It wasn't just shock or relief. That same man was . . . was . . .'

Even though she'd already explained all this to Jenny on the phone, Morven was finding it hard to say the words. 'He was the man who killed my parents.'

'Are you absolutely sure?' Jenny said. 'Stress and fear can do strange things to your brain.'

Morven had been asking herself the same thing but she had never been more sure of anything in her life. She nodded, warming her hands on the mug as she sat hunched over it.

'Well, finish your drink, quickly,' Jenny said. 'There'll be officers here soon to take your statement.'

Morven drained the last of the hot, sweet drink. She was starting to feel incredibly tired, as if she couldn't possibly keep her eyes open. Now Jenny was helping her up and guiding her to the bedroom. Telling her to lie down and have a little rest. But what about the NCA officers? The statement?

Everything went black.

Jenny looked down at Morven and shook her head sadly. It should never have come to this. As she had earlier, she wandered around the apartment looking at the paintings. But this time she selected the most valuable of them and took them down from the wall, making a small pile of framed pictures near the front door. She knew she had plenty of time. There were no NCA officers on the way. Maybe there would have been if Jenny had actually put in a report.

When she was satisfied that she had selected enough paintings Jenny returned to the bedroom. Morven was still unconscious and would be for some time, thanks to the narcotics Jenny had slipped into her hot chocolate.

However Jenny had come to the conclusion that drugging Morven wasn't enough. As soon as she came round, she would work out what Jenny had done and raise the alarm. No — there was only one way for Jenny to continue to get away with this.

She picked up a pillow from the other side of the bed and held it above Morven's face.

13

By the time the police were able to contact air traffic control to ask them to prevent the Khalil jet from taking off, it was too late. The plane had departed five minutes earlier.

However, a call to the dispatchers provided the information that one passenger had been left behind. Mrs Yasmeen Khalil was now in the security office at the airport.

When she was interviewed by two of Dave Bradley's officers at the police station later she admitted her involvement in the sham kidnapping of her daughter — intended as her way of escaping the control of her husband and his family.

The officers who interviewed her were surprised there was no fancy lawyer present but Yasmeen knew she would have to get used to life with no money. And whatever punishment she received from the legal system would be nothing compared to the loss of her child.

When Yasmeen had told Morven Jennings about what had led to the kidnap plot, she had led her to believe that Ayesha was not her husband's child. But Yasmeen had known the truth all along. No amount of wishing or hoping that Ayesha was actually John's child could have made it true.

Hamid had been certain of it, too, from the day their child was born. His obsessive need to be in control had led him to order the doctors to carry out a battery of tests on their newborn including DNA testing. He had known from day one that he was Ayesha's father.

Yasmeen sometimes wondered what he would have done if that test had come back negative but the thought of it always gave her nightmares. She was already well aware of what her husband and his family were capable of if their honour was in question.

Hamid would return to his comfortable life in Dubai and his family wealth would allow him to construct a story around these events that would leave him looking like a hero. Meanwhile Yasmeen would face the British justice system and then what? She hadn't seen John Whitehouse since their brief reunion at his brother's home. The pressure of their plan going wrong and the prospect of his political career being in ruins had changed him beyond recognition.

'How could we have been so naïve, Yasmeen?' he'd asked her. They were in the sitting room, with Ayesha playing happily in her travel cot.

When they had first seen each other an hour ago they had clung to each other and kissed passionately. That was how it was meant to have been. John had found a place where Yasmeen and Ayesha could stay hidden until the police investigation into their disappearance faded away. He had all the right contacts to obtain new identities for them both. Eventually they would be a family together.

While he was still in the public eye

Yasmeen would have to stay out of sight, but she was used to that by now. They were planning ahead to a time when John was no longer an MP and the three of them could live an anonymous life.

Then things had started to go terribly wrong. First, of course, was the death of the airport worker during Ayesha's abduction. Neither of them had realised how heavily that would lie on their consciences. Then tonight, instead of bringing Yasmeen alone to Newmarket, those two idiots had brought along an extra passenger — a police officer, of all people. Slowly but surely John and Yasmeen's plan was crumbling.

Yasmeen could tell just by looking into his eyes that he had already made a decision.

'It's time to be realistic, my love,' he said. 'This isn't going to end well. I was stupid to think it ever could. I'll try to take on most of the blame — it was my idea, after all. But if they work out that you were involved at all, they might charge you with conspiracy. You might get a short sentence but I'm going to lose everything, including my freedom, for many years.

'I don't want you to wait for me. I want you to go back to Dubai with Hamid. Oh, I know it goes against everything we've ever wished for — but at least he will provide for you and for Ayesha.'

Yasmeen was crying by now. This dream had kept her going for so long and now it looked as if she was going to have to crawl back to her husband and try to keep up the pretence that she had been kidnapped as well as Ayesha.

She didn't know how long she could put up with that, but at least their life of luxury was some compensation. The more she thought about the idea, the more she realised it was her only option.

'I'm going to contact my solicitor,' John said. 'Get him to come with me to the police. If I hand myself in I might get a lighter sentence in the end.' His face gave away the fact that he was struggling to come to terms with the prospect of losing his prestigious life and his freedom.

How soon things change, Yasmeen thought. From passionate kisses to a practical solution in such a short time.

'But what should I do if they've worked out I'm involved?' she said. 'PC Jennings knows — she'll tell them the minute she's freed.'

'By the time she's convinced them you were in on it rather than an innocent victim, you'll be out of their reach. Think about it — what is your husband going to do the minute he finds out you and Ayesha have been found?'

Yasmeen thought for a moment.

'He'll come for us and whisk us back off to Dubai,' she said, realising that John was right. Now she could see a way out of this situation she felt better. She surprised herself at how quickly she had started to look ahead rather than feeling distraught over the end of her relationship with John. Maybe it had all been built on a naïve dream after all.

John reached for his phone and scrolled through the contacts to find his solicitor. He wasn't a criminal lawyer, but he would be able to recommend one of the best.

Before the call had connected there was the sound of a gunshot outside, followed by the front door bursting open and someone running up the stairs. John didn't realise it, but at that moment his chance to give himself up at the police station had just been snatched away.

Now, sitting alone in a bare cell at the custody suite, Yasmeen reflected on how two chances of happiness had been taken from her in a few hours. Self-pity took away the twinges of guilt she had felt earlier about the death of the airport worker. A tear ran down her cheek as she sat, defeated, waiting to hear what her fate would be.

* * *

The jet carrying Hamid Khalil and his daughter, Ayesha, landed in Dubai and a limo was waiting to whisk them to their luxurious home. Hamid hadn't given a thought to how his wife was coping. She would soon be his ex-wife and of no interest to him.

He had spent much of the flight working out the practicalities of suddenly becoming the single parent of a year-old child. Within an hour of arriving home, he had organised a nanny to start work the next day. Main problem sorted. When money was no object, this sort of thing was simple.

Next on his list was a little more awkward. However he knew it would be better to initiate the conversation than to wait for his uncle to contact him.

'Thank you for allowing me to use the plane again so soon,' Hamid said when his call was answered. 'I am once again so very grateful.'

'Hamid, you know I am always here to help my brother's children,' his uncle replied. 'But there is something you need to understand. This . . . situation has affected our family's reputation.'

'I know, and I apologise,' Hamid said. It was vitally important to placate his uncle who could cut him off on a whim. This was turning into one of the most frightening conversations of Hamid's life. His horse training business, his home, his wealth — all of it depended on his uncle's favour.

'We still have a chance to rescue the situation,' his uncle said. He had apparently decided that Hamid had suffered enough. 'It will mean blackening the reputation of your, er, former wife even further. Once the gossip mongers in our social circle get hold of it they will have great pleasure spreading it far and wide.'

Hamid smiled and wiped the beads of sweat that had gathered earlier in the conversation from his brow. He'd been grateful for his family connections all his life, but never more than at this moment. Instead of coming out of this situation humiliated by a cheating wife, he might even end up looking like a hero who had rescued his child.

* * *

The difference between life and death can sometimes come down to just a few moments. If Jenny had remained undisturbed, pressing the pillow over Morven's unconscious face, for much longer it would have been too late.

Sergeant Foster burst into the room and with the element of surprise was able to overpower Jenny in seconds. It helped that the police officer's main leisure activity was martial arts.

She had Jenny face down on the floor with her hands cuffed behind her back before the other woman could make sense of what was happening.

The sergeant's next priority was to check on Morven. As she approached the bed, she feared for a moment that she hadn't made it in time, but then she saw Morven's chest rising and falling. She felt for a pulse and was relieved to find it slow but strong.

She phoned for an ambulance and then to the police station for a support team. This was now a crime scene — thankfully only attempted murder.

Morven had left a message on Sergeant Foster's voicemail just before she managed to contact Jenny. She hadn't given her all the details of her encounter with her parents' killer, but enough for the sergeant to decide it was too serious to ignore.

Morven had also had the foresight to give Sergeant Foster the codes for the building and it was probably this that had enabled her to save Morven's life. The minutes she would have spent outside trying to gain entry could have made all the difference.

On her way over, Sergeant Foster had tried to alert Dave Bradley to what was happening. She wasn't blind. She'd noticed the chemistry between the boss and PC Jennings. Not known for being romantic, she nevertheless had a soft spot for the pair of them. If a bit of drama could bring them together, why not?

* * *

Ben Gill had been waiting in a room in the custody suite at the police station for hours. His palms were sweaty and his pulse rate was starting to worry him.

If this is what it's like to be brought in for questioning when you know you've done nothing wrong, what must it feel like if you're actually guilty? he wondered.

Two police officers had turned up at his office asking to speak to him. They wouldn't tell him what it was about — just 'helping with an ongoing enquiry'. On the way to the station Ben had decided it must be something to do with one of his clients but then, once they'd arrived, he was told he would be questioned under caution and asked if he wanted a solicitor present.

That was when it became clear that it was something to do with Morven Jennings.

After that, everything had gone downhill quickly. Ben still didn't understand what he was supposed to have done but it apparently involved his cousin, Paula. When he worked out that he was suspected, along with Paula, of attempting to steal money from Morven's bank accounts, Ben was horrified.

'I need to speak to my supervisor at the National Crime Agency,' he told the officer in charge of the interview. If he'd hoped to impress anyone by mentioning he worked at the NCA he was mistaken.

Ben whispered to his solicitor that answering any further questions could compromise a case he was assigned to and the interview was suspended.

Now Ben was in limbo while the police and the NCA negotiated how to take things further. He looked around the stark room and an icy fear gripped him. Up to this point in his life, things had been going pretty well. He'd done OK at school, scraped an average degree after enjoying his student years and landed a decent job compared to most of his mates.

Out of nowhere Ben could see his

career and his future crumbling away. From the questions he'd been asked earlier he could tell that, somehow, the police had evidence that he'd organised whatever had happened at Morven's bank.

He wasn't naïve enough to believe that innocent people were never convicted of crimes.

Right now, he certainly wished he could believe that his innocence would be enough to guarantee that this nightmare would soon be over. Instead, he had a sinking feeling in his heart that his one stupid mistake, trying to help his cousin get her life back on track, was going to ruin his own life.

* * *

Paula Gill had been released on police bail having been charged with fraud and attempted theft. She knew she couldn't return to Morven's apartment so her only option was to go to her parents' home with her tail between her legs.

She was dreading the reception she

would get. According to a text her mum had sent minutes earlier, Ben, the golden boy of the family, was still in custody. He'd probably already lost his job but things would be a million times worse if the police managed to make any of the charges stick.

When Paula was being interviewed, the police officer had let a few hints about the evidence against Ben slip into the conversation. Apparently there was stuff on his work computer that incriminated him.

Well, Paula knew who would have put that there. Jenny Mason was a frightening woman and Paula realised now just how far under Jenny's spell she had been.

Paula hadn't coped well with being locked up at the police station in between interviews. If that was a taste of what being in prison was like, she didn't think she'd survive it.

Her court-appointed solicitor advised her to plead guilty but Paula was worried about the impact of her previous behaviour when she had been given an

ASBO for damaging her ex's property and harassing his wife.

The solicitor was still sure that admitting to what she had done this time was the best course of action. Considering her age and the relatively minor previous offences he was predicting that she'd be given a community service sentence.

But what about Ben? she wondered. Paula knew he was completely innocent. The only thing he'd done wrong was to cover up the fact that he'd helped Paula to find somewhere to live. Somewhere that was against the rules of his job.

The closer Paula came to her parents' house the slower she walked. Deep down she knew the right thing to do — but could she bring herself to actually do it?

Right now she was looking at being able to walk away from this with barely a slap on the wrist. But surely anyone with a conscience would want to make sure their cousin was released and was able to clear his name.

For the first time she could remember, that idea didn't seem ridiculous to

Paula. All her life she had looked out for number one regardless of the consequences for others. Whenever she'd done anything wrong when she was growing up her first instinct had been to deny it and then look around for someone to blame.

Her only serious relationship, the one that had almost wrecked her life only last year, had been based on a lie by her lover. Her reaction when she found out he was married had been totally out of proportion to what had been done to her. She'd damaged property and, if she hadn't been stopped, might have gone on to harm a person who was blameless.

No matter what she had done, Paula had always been able to find a way of shifting the blame from herself to someone else, even if it was only in her own mind. Now she was starting to doubt the value of her self-centred attitude to life for the first time ever.

She turned round and headed back to the police station. She would give a new statement explaining that Ben had nothing to do with the crime — and setting out exactly who was responsible. If that led to consequences later when Jenny Mason was released from what was sure to be a prison sentence, Paula would deal with it then.

A new feeling took its place in Paula's heart. It took her a few minutes to realise what it was — she was proud of herself.

⋆ ⋆ ⋆

Jenny Mason had maintained an ice-cold exterior the whole time she had been in police custody, but on the inside she was a cauldron of anxiety and insecurity.

Right from the start of her questioning she had decided to stay silent — it was her right, as they'd told her when she was arrested.

So after a while she had simply stopped listening, concentrating instead on the subject that was now occupying her every thought. Her child.

How could she have let things get so out of hand, to the point where there was every likelihood she would lose her daughter forever?

She could probably have walked away from the fraud, conspiracy and attempted theft charges after a short spell in prison. Her sister might have been willing to look after the baby for a while. But Jenny had to admit, to herself if not to the police, that she had lost control when it came to Morven Jennings.

She'd been on her way over to Morven's apartment to remove some more valuables, when she received Morven's call. She'd spent hours working out how she could get away with several paintings without anyone being able to lay the blame on her.

Getting into the building and the apartment wouldn't have been a problem — she still knew the access codes she'd been given when she was working with Morven. If they'd been changed, well, she'd find a way round it — she was nothing if not resourceful. And then Morven rang, desperate for help because her parents' killer had appeared.

Briefly annoyed that her plan to steal the art works was not going to be possible, Jenny quickly saw a new opportunity. She calmed Morven down and assured her she would come round as soon as possible. She'd patted her jacket pocket and smiled to herself. Of course she realised now, looking back, that normal people don't carry strong sleeping tablets around with them as a way of being prepared for every eventuality. But at the time, she had congratulated herself on being oh, so clever.

Jenny couldn't pinpoint exactly when the line between rational behaviour and what she had ended up doing had become blurred. It was almost as if she'd been on autopilot, only brought back to her senses when the policewoman arrived and knocked her to the floor. The memory brought to mind the fact that Jenny's back was hurting terribly, but she sensed there wouldn't be much sympathy for someone who'd tried to kill one of these officers' colleagues.

For the first time in a long while, Jenny thought about another situation where things had got out of hand. Her relationship with Morven wasn't the only time her management of a client's case had slipped over the line into being overfamiliar.

Jenny almost laughed to herself at that term because it came nowhere near to describing her short-lived relationship with her baby's father.

While her feelings towards Morven had been descending into envy and bitterness, she had meanwhile taken on the case of a man in his forties who had turned himself in to police offering evidence against a drugs gang in exchange for protection. From the moment she met him, Jenny had been smitten.

She knew she should have gone to her supervisor straight away and asked to be taken off the case. It had happened to some of her colleagues before, and it would happen again. But Jenny had been dissatisfied with her life and her job for so long, she ignored what all her training and experience had taught her and carried on regardless.

She didn't know if he felt the same for her or whether he simply saw seducing her as a challenge, but it wasn't long before they ended up sleeping together. And whether her lack of taking precautions was because she hadn't expected things to move so quickly, or whether it was out of a subconscious desire to have a child, Jenny found out she was pregnant a few weeks later.

When she asked for a meeting with her supervisor and asked for the case to be reassigned, Jenny was aware that the damage was done, but she had thought long and hard about the man she had put her livelihood at risk for. Even if he hadn't been a client, he was the worst candidate for fatherhood she had ever met.

She hadn't seen him since that day and she had made sure he had no idea he had fathered her child. The space for the father's name on her baby's birth certificate was blank. When the time came to explain it to her daughter, she simply planned to tell her they had split up before she was born and lost touch with each other.

Once again Jenny's thoughts homed in on the future for her baby. Attempted murder meant a long sentence. It was almost certain her child would be taken into care. There was no way Jenny's sister would take her on long-term and they had no close family apart from each other.

Jenny knew that the best thing for the child would be adoption. There were plenty of people out there waiting to give a home to a baby.

Tears began to fall onto the scratched table in front of Jenny. The officer asking the questions glanced at Jenny's solicitor and declared a break.

'I want to plead guilty to all charges,' Jenny said to her solicitor when they were left alone.

'Don't be too hasty,' he said. 'There

are mitigating circumstances we can look into. Post natal depression, that sort of thing.'

'Undiagnosed until I found myself under arrest? I don't think I'd get away with that.' Jenny gave a humourless laugh. 'I've worked on enough criminal cases to have seen all the tricks. The only thing that matters to me now is for my child to have a happy life. I want her put up for adoption. One thing I want you to fight for — I need to be able to see my child as she grows up.'

The solicitor nodded and went to find the officer who'd been dealing with them. If his client was as clued up on the legal system as she thought she was, she would have realised what she was asking for was impossible.

* * *

The combination of Paula changing her statement about the bank fraud and Jenny admitting to all charges meant that Ben Gill was released from custody without charge. He was shell-shocked but so relieved to be free that he set off home with a spring in his step.

It wasn't long, though, before his cheery mood was spoiled. Scrolling through the messages on the phone that had just been returned to him, he found one from his manager requesting a meeting first thing the following morning.

Ben realised he was going to have to explain why his cousin had been lodging at the home of one of his clients. Was it a sackable offence? Probably. It had certainly been stupidity.

There was nothing he could do about it for now except hope his manager would give him another chance. They were so short-staffed it wasn't a completely impossible idea.

* * *

The door buzzer was the last thing Morven wanted to hear. She'd finally managed to fall asleep on one of the sofas but the annoying buzzing wouldn't go away. Having insisted on being discharged from hospital in the early hours and come home by taxi, she'd tried to go to bed as normal but the thought of what had happened in her bedroom — how close she'd come to dying — had prevented her.

The room had been left in quite a mess by the CSI team too, which hadn't helped. How could they cause so much disruption investigating someone having a pillow put over their face?

Sergeant Foster had told Morven some of the details when she regained consciousness from the drugs. Jenny Mason had been arrested and the police team the sergeant had called in had found another suspect in the apartment block grounds. He had been identified as Lee Robertson, a member of the armed response team who covered the Newmarket area. He was currently being treated for the damage Morven's pepper spray had done to his face.

Morven knew she would have to make a statement at some point, explaining where Jenny Mason and Lee Robertson fitted into her complicated life. But for now Sergeant Foster had told her to rest.

As soon as the sergeant had left, Morven was pestering the medical staff to allow her to go home.

Thinking about her bedroom again, Morven decided she was going to have to do one of her obsessive cleaning sessions. Or strip the room of everything and replace it all.

For the first time another thought crept in — maybe it was time to think about moving out and finding somewhere else to live. Her memories of this apartment were no longer good.

The buzzer *again* — whoever it was, they were persistent. Morven finally went to answer it, peering at the video screen. She couldn't see who it was because they were hidden by a huge bouquet of flowers.

Dave? *Don't be stupid*, she told herself. After the rude way she had cancelled their date he was hardly likely to turn up carrying flowers.

'Who is it?' she said.

'Hi, Morven, it's me,' a voice answered. Then, realising they couldn't be seen by the camera, the person shifted the bouquet to one side.

It was her personal banker, Jacob. Morven buzzed him in.

While he was travelling up in the lift Morven brushed her hair in an attempt to make herself look more presentable, then flicked on the kettle to make them both tea.

'Hi, Jacob,' she said. 'Well, this is a first — a home visit. New service?'

Jacob gave her a sheepish smile.

'They called me in from leave to come and give our abject apologies for your accounts being accessed online.'

'No, it's I who should be apologising,' Morven said. 'First, there's no way your bosses should have cut short your holiday to deal with me, and second, I must have left my laptop insecure for my flatmate to find. If anything, I should be thanking the bank for acting on my instructions so swiftly.'

'To tell you the truth,' Jacob said, 'I wasn't that upset at being called in — the kids were driving me mad.'

They both laughed.

An idea had been starting to form in Morven's mind — a grand plan that Jacob and the bank could help her with. Over tea and biscuits, she tentatively shared her idea to see what Jacob thought of her plans.

* * *

Morven was signed off work after her drugging ordeal, on top of everything else she'd been through in the past week. The doctor had told her to take a few days off, but she knew she would never be going back.

The man she had been searching for since her parents were killed was now in custody. There would be no point in her carrying on as a super recogniser now her main motivation had gone.

She had phoned Sergeant Foster the

previous day to thank her for rescuing her and to tell her that she had decided to leave the police force.

'Sergeant, I can't express how grateful I am to you for all you've done,' she said.

'I think after all we've been through, we can be on first name terms, don't you?' the sergeant had said. 'Call me Elizabeth from now on, even if I can't convince you to reconsider your decision on leaving.'

Morven had thought long and hard about it. She knew the super recogniser role helped to put away criminals and therefore helped victims of crime. Yet she also knew that she wasn't exceptional, as far as super recognisers go. In due course Elizabeth would find a replacement who would be at least as good.

Morven had been thinking for a while about a way she could put her money to good use. She planned to set up an organisation to support victims of violent crime and their relatives — especially young people who had lost family members.

She told her former supervisor a little about her idea.

'Morven, that's a fantastic idea,' she said warmly. 'I can't think of anyone better placed to help those victims. Good for you. And if you need any help just shout — I'd love to be involved.'

Morven felt a warm glow at being reminded that there were good people in the world. She started to try to bring the conversation to a close as she could feel another headache coming on, but Elizabeth interrupted.

'Just one other thing,' she said. 'There's a certain DI here who's making everyone's lives a complete misery — apparently because you won't return his calls.'

Morven sighed.

'It's complicated, Elizabeth. I thought we had something but I refuse to be anyone's second choice.'

'What are you talking about?'

'We've come close to getting together but each time his girlfriend shows up.

I'm not going to be the other woman, no matter how much I'm attracted to someone.'

There, she'd admitted it to someone who knew them both at last. The only time she'd spoken about her feelings for Dave before had been to Paula Gill. Morven shuddered at the memory of thinking she had a friend.

Elizabeth thought for a moment.

'This girlfriend — is she blonde and drives a blue hatchback?'

'Yes, that's her.'

Elizabeth tried to stop herself laughing but it was no good.

'That's Dave's kid sister, Anne,' she said. 'Fusses about him like a mother hen. Always bringing him clean shirts and meals in Tupperware.'

Morven's reaction was mixed. She felt stupid for jumping to the conclusion that Dave was in a relationship despite what he'd said to her. But mostly she felt elated. She couldn't wait to get Elizabeth off the phone so she could ring him. They said goodbye,

Morven assuring Elizabeth that she would meet her for coffee soon.

Now the time had come to talk to Dave, Morven suddenly felt like an awkward teenager. Probably because since she was in her teens, she'd never had a relationship that had lasted for long. When anyone showed an interest Morven had always put them off, either intentionally or subconsciously. She was always afraid to be close to anyone for fear that her true identity would be revealed or that her past history would put the other person at risk. It was a lonely life at times — but it was what she was used to.

Dave Bradley was the first man to make her think seriously about changing her attitude to relationships. She'd been ready to take a chance on love with Dave even before her parents' killer had been arrested.

It hadn't been fear of her past that had stopped her wanting to get closer to Dave. It had been her belief that he already had a girlfriend. Now that

Elizabeth Foster had put her straight on that score, Morven was determined to find out if Dave was really interested in her.

Having rushed Elizabeth off the phone so she could call him, she now thought of a dozen things that needed doing before she could speak to him. She reached for her phone and put it back repeatedly, so it was over an hour later when she finally pulled herself together and made the call.

It'll go to voicemail, she thought to herself, *it always does*. But not this time. For once Dave picked up and his phone screen showed him who was calling.

'Morven, hi,' he said. 'How are you?'

The concern was obvious in his voice.

'I'm OK,' she said, then took a deep breath. It was time to jump in with both feet. 'Listen, I've just been talking to Sergeant Foster. Elizabeth. I'm assuming it's common knowledge by now that I'm leaving?'

Morven knew Elizabeth would have had to set the wheels in motion to replace Morven in her team, and a tasty piece of gossip like that would spread through the station like wildfire.

'Yeah, I'd heard,' Dave said.

A silence stretched between them, too long to be comfortable. Then of course they both spoke at once.

'She said that — '

'Listen, Morven how about — '

They laughed and Morven insisted Dave should go first.

'OK, I was just going to ask if we could try again and have that meal we talked about.'

Morven cringed when she remembered the abrupt message she'd left cancelling their date.

'I think that's a great idea,' she said. 'I'm free tonight if . . . '

'Brilliant. What were you going to say before I interrupted?' Dave wanted to know.

'It's just that Elizabeth said you'd mentioned I wasn't returning your calls. I thought I should explain.'

'There's no need,' Dave said. 'You've

been through an awful time of it. I should've backed off until you'd had time to deal with it.'

'It wasn't that,' Morven said. 'Oh, I feel so stupid having to admit this.'

'What?' Dave was worried now.

'I thought you had a girlfriend,' Morven said, imagining how odd this must sound. 'I'd seen you with the same woman a few times and I thought you just wanted me as a bit on the side. Elizabeth told me she's your sister.'

'Anne?' Dave laughed. 'Yes, she's my fussy, over-protective sister who thinks I can't wash my own clothes or feed myself. Though I must say it comes in handy when she offers to pick me up from the pub when I've had a few.'

'As soon as I knew who she was I realised how silly I'd been,' Morven said.

'Well, to be fair she is around a lot at the moment,' Dave said. 'Our dad's been in hospital for a few weeks. It was touch and go for a while and Anne was picking me up to go and visit him whenever

I could get away. In the meantime she's been around even more than usual — I suppose a psychologist would say the fear of losing Dad has made her worry about me more.'

Morven was feeling pretty guilty by now. She hadn't even considered that Anne might have so much on her mind.

'Anyway,' Dave said. 'I'm glad you've told me. I was worrying that you weren't returning my calls because I'd been wrong to think there might be something special between us.'

'You weren't wrong,' Morven said, then kicked herself for not exactly playing hard to get. But now she'd got everything off her chest she felt much happier.

She was going to do her best to break the habit of a lifetime and stop overthinking her relationship with Dave. She knew she needed to give it a chance and let things develop at their own pace.

That didn't stop her sitting and daydreaming long after they'd disconnected their call. Was it her turn for some happiness at last?

First things first — ever the practical one, Morven reached for a notepad and started making a shopping list. The first meal she cooked for Dave Bradley was going to be memorable. And hopefully the first of many, many more.

* * *

For the third time in ten minutes Morven checked that everything was ready for the meal she'd prepared so carefully. The dining table was set, a candle waiting to be lit. *Too much?* she wondered and moved it onto a nearby shelf. Then she moved it back again. *Get a grip*, she kept telling herself. Maybe she should have agreed to go out to a restaurant after all. But no. The most important thing to her at the moment was to maintain some sort of control over her life and her choices. The last few days had left her feeling decidedly insecure.

Dave was due to arrive soon and Morven realised she hadn't even changed her clothes. She'd spent hours bouncing between the kitchen and the rest of the apartment, alternating between preparing the meal and virtually spring-cleaning every room.

Every room, that is, apart from the one where Paula Gill had stayed. Her belongings were still there, with the door firmly closed on them so Morven could postpone deciding what to do with them.

Part of her would have liked to throw the lot into one of the large bins outside, but she knew she wouldn't. For now, she would wait and see whether Paula was brave enough to contact her to ask for her things back. Paula had always seemed like a very confident, assertive person but Morven wasn't sure she'd ever really known her at all.

Strangely there was a part of Morven that was grateful to Paula Gill. She had taught her a lesson she would never forget, about how easy it could be to be fooled by someone. But mostly she felt hurt that someone she had considered a friend could have treated her so badly.

And as for Jenny Mason — Morven's feelings about Jenny were too complicated to be unravelled yet. For now, she was glad the justice system was dealing with Jenny. A senior manager at the National Crime Agency had contacted Morven earlier.

'An enquiry has been set up into what happened,' she said. 'And I'm assigning you a new liaison officer.'

'If the man who was arrested here is convicted of my parents' murders,' Morven said, 'I think I'm going to want to leave your protection.'

'Well, I'll set up a meeting for you with the new liaison officer anyway and we'll see how things go.'

After that conversation Morven sat for a while and thought about the future. She hadn't really considered the possibility of leaving witness protection before, but the idea was growing on her. Until recently the system had done nothing but good for her, but she liked the thought of making her own decisions about her life.

She hurried to her room and changed into the outfit she'd spent an hour choosing earlier. She hoped the black jeans and green silk top achieved the 'not trying too hard' look she was aiming for.

Morven glanced at the clock and frowned. He was late. Just as she started to think he might have changed his mind, the buzzer sounded and the screen showed Dave Bradley standing at the main door clutching a bottle of wine.

Her heart did a flip as she pressed the button to open the door.

'Something smells amazing,' Dave said as he followed her through to the kitchen.

'Oh, it's nothing special,' she said, as if she cooked gourmet meals every night of the week.

A silence hung between them. Morven felt her lack of relationships experience more than ever.

'Drink?' she asked, taking the bottle from Dave and noting the above-average label.

'Just one,' he said. 'Driving.'

Well, at least he didn't expect to stay

over after their first evening together. Morven couldn't decide whether she was pleased or disappointed.

She sent Dave to wait in the sitting room while she got the food ready to serve. He took the opportunity to check out her bookcases and DVD preferences, neither of which gave much away about her. The speakers were giving out a playlist of recent soft rock music.

'It's ready,' Morven called and Dave joined her at the dining table.

The food tasted as wonderful as it had smelled but at first the conversation was stilted and uncomfortable. Morven had decided earlier to tell Dave everything about her background. Now they were struggling to find topics of conversation, she decided it was the perfect time.

'You must have been wondering how I can afford to live in a place like this,' she said.

'None of my business,' Dave said, though the curiosity was obvious on his face.

'Well, I want you to know. I lost both my parents when I was a teenager. My dad ran a successful business and I was left — well, a fortune I suppose, in their wills.'

Dave nodded. A pretty simple explanation, but he was sure there was more to it. As Morven carried on with her story he was proved right.

'I was only sixteen so my Uncle Adam, Adam McLean, became my guardian. He wasn't my real uncle but as good as. He and his wife were my parents' closest friends. I remember how they used to come round to our house for meals and when I was little I'd sit on the stairs, trying to listen to their conversations. Anyway, they took me in and looked after me for a while, but because of the, er, circumstances of my parents' deaths that arrangement didn't last for long.'

'Circumstances?' Dave asked gently.

Morven tried to work out the best way to say the next part. She didn't want to end up in tears as she usually did, reliving that awful night.

'Both my parents were murdered. Shot. I was there and I saw the killer.' Morven was rushing the words out so she didn't have to concentrate on them for too long. 'Uncle Adam arranged for me to go into the Protected Persons scheme.'

'Witness protection?' Dave's eyes widened.

'Exactly,' Morven said.

'So you're not really Morven Jennings?'

'Well, I am now. I used to be called Elly Clarke. My mum and dad were James and Eva Clarke.' Morven's voice almost broke at this point but she managed to pull herself together and stop herself from giving in to tears.

Dave thought for a moment.

'I remember the case. I think it was when I was in police training college but I definitely remember seeing it in the papers and on TV.'

Morven took a deep breath.

'Well, that's me. But if it's OK I'd rather not talk about it any more for now.'

Dave had a hundred questions about

what he'd just heard, but he respected Morven's feelings. They were back to an awkward silence, so at last Dave decided to address the elephant in the room.

'Morven, I can't keep sidestepping what's going on here,' he said.

Morven put her glass down and stared into his eyes. If what he said next wasn't something that confirmed he felt the same for her as she did towards him, she would give up.

'When I heard you were leaving the force it was such a relief,' he continued.

Uh oh, Morven thought. Where was this going?

He carried on, 'It's been the only thing stopping me from asking you out. Relationships between higher and lower ranks in the same department aren't allowed. One of us would've had to leave and now that you're going anyway . . .'

Morven's laugh stopped him in his tracks. Was she laughing at the idea of a relationship with him? But Morven reached across the table and took his hand.

'You don't know how long I've waited to hear you say you wanted to ask me out,' she said, once again failing at the hard-to-get thing.

The food forgotten, they stood and moved into each other's arms.

A buzzing in Dave's pocket interrupted them before their embrace progressed any further. He knew he didn't need to explain or apologise to Morven for taking the call. But once he'd listened for a moment, his expression became anxious and he was already reaching for his jacket as he disconnected the call.

'It's my dad,' he said. 'Taken a turn for the worse. I'll have to go. If it had been work I would've told them to sort it out themselves, but this . . . '

'No, of course you must go,' Morven said. She of all people knew how important parents were.

* * *

A couple of hours later Dave texted to let her know his dad was stabilised and he'd phone her tomorrow. She settled down under a quilt on a sofa, wondering if they were destined never to spend a whole evening, or night, together.

14

Even a week on from all the drama, there were still a few things Morven didn't understand. She had asked Dave to arrange a meeting with the senior officer on her parents' killer's case. What was the point of knowing people on the inside if she didn't make use of it?

And Dave had kept asking her to tell him if there was anything he could help with. He had insisted on being a go-between rather than Morven involving herself in the case herself.

'It would only need one slip up for Robertson's lawyer to find away to get him off on a technicality,' he said. 'You know I'm right. Let me take the DI on the case out for a few beers. That way it'll all be off the record.'

Morven saw the sense in this argument right away. If the case against

Robertson collapsed at this point, she didn't think she could handle it. They agreed that Dave would take his colleague out that evening, then come and report back to her. She couldn't help thinking that it was a better idea all round. She'd find out what she needed to know and then . . . well, then it might be time to move her relationship with Dave up a level.

He was as good as his word, turning up in a taxi just after nine that evening. He wasn't drunk but Morven could tell he was more relaxed than usual. Once he'd settled down on one of the sofas Morven sat on the other one, elbows on her knees, impatient to hear what he'd learned.

'Well, first of all, confirmation of what we already thought we knew,' Dave said. 'Lee Robertson was hired to kill your parents. The forensic financial guys have tracked his accounts back ten years and found a number of large payments. It looks as though he's responsible for a number of unsolved contract killings going back fifteen to twenty years. Strangely, after your parents' murders it looks like he tried to go straight. And because he'd never been caught for any crimes he was able to join the police force.'

'I thought they did incredibly detailed background checks,' Morven said. 'I know that was a concern when I applied. That my witness protection status would be compromised.'

'You're right. There are checks into family background, finances, all that stuff. But in Robertson's case there was nothing to find. He had an everyday job, unremarkable family links. He must have simply forgotten to mention his part-time job as an assassin.' Dave was trying to lighten the tone of the conversation but he could tell from Morven's expression that he'd miscalculated. 'Sorry,' he said, taking her hand.

'OK, so so he's been in the police for years. What about more recently?' Morven asked. The irony of the man who'd gunned down her parents being paid by the police force to use a gun every day was weighing heavily on her. 'How did he happen to show up where I live, just after I'd unwittingly recognised him in Newmarket? Surely he wasn't in on John Whitehouse's plot?'

'It seems it was just a coincidence that he was part of that unit that arrested the kidnappers. But while you didn't realise at the time that you'd seen him before, he recognised you from the newspaper coverage of your parents' deaths. Photos of you and your parents were plastered over the front pages for days after the murders.

'Although 'Elly' disappeared off the face of the earth a short time later, those pictures can still be found on the internet. He panicked, thinking that you could ruin the life he's built for himself over the past ten years. He saw you get into my car and when his unit returned to headquarters in their van, he spotted you waiting for me.

'He followed us to London in his own car and . . . you know the rest.'

Morven nodded, processing everything Dave had told her so far before urging him to carry on.

'This next bit's not going to be easy to hear.' He sighed and hoped he could find the right words to soften the blow. 'You must be wondering who hired Robertson,' he said.

Morven nodded, her eyes not leaving his for a second.

'You told me it was always assumed that your dad had evidence of illegal deals that would incriminate someone. Well, the team has investigated the deals he was involved with again and, together with the payments to Lee Robertson, they had enough evidence to arrest someone today.'

'Who?' Morven asked.

'Morven, I'm sorry to have to tell you it's Adam McLean.'

'Uncle Adam?' Morven felt as if her world had ended for the second time in a couple of weeks. First, her supposed protector Jenny Mason had betrayed her. Now the person she had credited with caring for her after her parents' deaths was responsible for their murders. It was too much.

'I just can't believe it,' she said, tears streaming down her face.

Dave moved next to her and took her in his arms, stroking her hair and waiting until the tears subsided. He'd known that the news would devastate her but also that he couldn't try to keep it from her. His pledge to keep Morven safe didn't mean hiding the truth.

Eventually Morven's mood changed from distress to anger and confusion.

'What I don't understand,' she said, 'is how come Uncle Adam arranged for me to go into witness protection? He knew I'd seen the killer. Why didn't he pay someone to get rid of me too?'

'I wondered that too,' Dave said. 'I think it's a bit like one of those old fairy tales. He needed you out of the way but he couldn't bring himself to kill a child. A child he'd known all her life. So instead he got rid of Elly Clarke without killing her.'

'A far-fetched theory for a tough police officer to come up with,' Morven said. 'But I like it.'

They stared into each other's eyes — he seeing the hurt he'd just inflicted dissolving, her searching for a clue as to where this might lead.

Their kiss, when it came at last, released the longing they'd both felt and that had been growing since the first time they met.

Dave knew that it would be the easiest thing in the world for him to carry Morven through to her bedroom. He also knew that he would feel as if he was taking advantage of her emotional state. As if she'd read his thoughts, Morven hugged him tightly.

'Thank you,' she said. 'For finding all this out and for telling me. It can't have been easy to pass on such awful news. And now I need some time to process it all. But Dave . . . '

'Yes?'

'Promise me we'll take up from where we're leaving off next time you come round. How about tomorrow night?'

'It's a date,' he said. 'And a promise.'

15

Lee Robertson was settling into his cell. He needed to keep his wits about him — there were plenty of men in this place with a score to settle with him. In his previous life he'd disposed of quite a few members of criminal families and gangs.

As well as being a very lucrative way to make a living, he saw it as doing a public service. Why should the public have to pay to keep criminals fed and sheltered in prison when it was so easy get rid of them altogether? Not a very politically correct attitude to life, he realised, but it had worked for him at that time.

He wasn't some kind of vigilante or superhero wannabe, though. His specialist services came at a high price. But once he was hired by someone with a burning desire to rid the world of a rival or a threat to them, he took a professional approach to the task.

As well as contract killing he was a renowned safe-cracker and he'd never been caught — never even close. So it was ironic that ten years after he'd decided on a change of career, it was an echo from his last job that had been his downfall.

That last client of his, Adam McLean, had been almost hysterical when he contacted Robertson after it all went wrong.

'You were only supposed to empty the safe and get rid of the contents!' he shouted.

'Not my fault you got the briefing wrong,' Lee had replied calmly. 'You always knew what I'd do if I was disturbed. I hope there won't be any delay in the second payment.'

He always demanded half his fee up front and the rest on completion. It'd always worked in the past. Clients were so grateful for his services. Well aware of his abilities, they weren't tempted to try and screw him over.

McLean had eventually calmed down and understood. His priority was to make sure nothing could be traced back to him. Lee had almost wished he'd kept hold of the precious contents of that safe — they may have come in useful in the future. But they were now lying in a skip on its way to landfill.

It wasn't until he read the papers next day that Lee realised there was an orphaned teenager left behind by the Clarkes. How had he not seen her? He got back in touch with McLean.

'Where's the girl?' he asked but McLean wasn't giving anything away.

'You've killed both her parents, wrecked her life — now leave her alone,' he said.

A few days later, Lee realised McLean had arranged for the Clarke kid to disappear. It was frustrating, but not the end of the world.

Still, the fiasco of that last job had caused Lee to reassess his life. For years he'd been stashing large amounts of money in an untraceable Swiss bank account. There was enough to provide for him, his wife and the kids for the rest of their lives.

After six months of doing very little, however, he realised that he needed to find some kind of job to replace the thrill he'd found in his contract killing work. As an armed police officer, he would still be using his sophisticated skills to take criminals off the street — just not quite so finally, most of the time.

However, having wiped out so many criminals years ago and then having moved over to the police force, Lee Robertson was now doubly a target in prison. His priority now was to pass on to his wife the codes and details required to access the Swiss bank money. Once he'd done that he'd take his chances with anyone who threatened him.

Visiting time was in an hour. The codes were all in his head, memorised — nothing written down which meant that nothing could be found by police searching his home.

As he made his way from his cell towards the door that led to the visiting room, Lee felt a shove that sent him tumbling down the metal staircase. Someone had seen their chance to give him a first warning of what his life in prison would be like. They didn't realise the knock he suffered to his head would do quite so much damage.

'The part of his brain that stores and retrieves certain memories has been affected,' the doctor told Lee's wife later. 'It's unlikely that it will ever be restored.'

* * *

Adam McLean was a broken man. A respected solicitor for most of his life, his fall from grace was hurting him badly. The only contact he'd had with his wife since his arrest was via her own solicitor. The marriage was over years ago and now she was going to make it official.

Of all the stupid things he'd done in his life, the chain of events he'd set in motion that led to James and Eva Clarke's deaths was the worst by far. Not a day went by that he didn't wish he'd never heard of Lee Robertson. Yet it was no use trying to lay all the blame at the feet of the hired criminal. It was Adam who had created the situation. And he had no excuses — it was sheer greed that had led him to set up the fraudulent deal that James Clarke had discovered.

That was the moment in time when Adam should have talked to his lifelong friend and asked for his help. Instead he had let things escalate until the only option James had been left with was to turn him in to the police, along with the evidence he'd gathered. Then Adam had panicked . . . and the rest was history.

No amount of trying to make things better by caring for Elly Clarke had worked. She was a constant reminder of what he'd done — and she was also at risk as long as Robertson could trace her through the McLeans. That was why Adam had contacted the witness protection people. He'd spent the ten years since trying to live a blame-free life as some sort of penance, but his marriage had become the latest victim.

Adam McLean was destined to spend many years in prison. There would be no family or friends to visit him. By the time he was released he would be a lonely old man — and he knew it was exactly what he deserved.

16

A month after the abduction of Ayesha Khalil, a quiet crowd of people gathered in the check-in hall from where she had been taken. Several of the major crime team attended, along with family and friends of Carly Simmonds.

Carly's dad tried to say a few words but his voice wavered and his wife went to stand next to him and put her arm around him.

They'd disagreed about attending this informal memorial at first. Carly had worked there for barely a couple of hours, after all. If she hadn't started work that day, she'd still be with them. But eventually they'd agreed it was important to remember how proud she'd been when she heard she'd got the job.

Some of the people gathered there were other airport workers who, although they hadn't known Carly because it was her first day, had felt strongly that they should pay their respects.

Everyone bowed their heads in silence for a few moments to think about the young woman who had been so excited to start work that day. With her whole life ahead of her, she should have returned to her parents' home that evening bursting with things to tell them about her day. Instead they'd had a visit from two police officers who told them she would never come home again.

In all the press coverage about the aftermath of the case, the biggest headlines had been about the disgrace of John Whitehouse MP. Carly only ever rated a couple of sentences when the case was mentioned.

The irony of this would have made the MP laugh had he not been at the lowest point of his life. He had put so much effort into publicising Ayesha's kidnapping, in an effort to convince Hamid Khalil that the crime was real. He knew that if Hamid had the slightest suspicion that the abduction was a sham, the full power of his family would have been brought in to punish Yasmeen and to find out who had helped her. The only way he could imagine convincing the Khalils was to keep a focus on Ayesha's disappearance in the press and on TV.

What he hadn't realised at the time was that it was not only the media but the police who were taking notice of him. Looking back, he could see that he should have kept a low profile — kept out of the way completely until Yasmeen and Ayesha were safely away from Hamid's clutches. Now that he wished the press would ignore him and the scandal he had brought upon himself, he was suddenly on all the front pages.

John had pleaded guilty to all charges when he appeared in court for the first time. He had failed in his attempt to create a new life with the woman he loved. The hardest thing he had ever done was to tell her to forget him and go back to her old life. Now all he could do was face his punishment

His cronies Matt Hanlon and Pete

Harris had pleaded guilty too, although both had tried to make a deal based on naming the men who had carried out the actual kidnapping. Those men had been picked up and were also looking at lengthy prison sentences.

Mark Whitehouse was the only one who looked likely to get off more lightly. The CPS were struggling to prove whether he knew the real reason behind him attending the hospice charity event in his brother's place.

It hadn't taken long for Sergeant Foster's team to point out that the man on the hospice CCTV was Mark Whitehouse, not his brother, but Mark's explanation that he thought he was simply covering for his brother double-booking himself was plausible. His only other involvement was that his premises had been used, but he had claimed he was forced into it by his brother.

Having been willing to give evidence against John and the others, including the nanny who had looked after Ayesha for the first few days after her disappearance, it looked as if he would be able to make a deal. In his own mind Mark was starting to look on the whole experience as doing him a favour. At long last, he was able to break the bond that had made him lie for his brother all his life. Still, whenever he remembered Carly Simmonds, he knew that no benefit to him could ever be worth someone's life.

Having been released on bail, Mark was now back at the stables. His solicitor had managed to convince the magistrates that Mark was a reputable business owner and highly unlikely to try to evade justice. Walking round the yard, surveying the animals and employees who made up his world, Mark knew he would never again risk losing all this — certainly not for his brother.

Mark's assistant had kept things ticking over and had done a great job. It was a relief to know that if he did end up serving time in prison, the place would be in good hands.

Mark had spent a lot of time while he

was in police custody pondering why he had covered up for his brother for so long. He'd come to the conclusion it was all tied up with his grief at losing his father. However he knew his dad would agree that it was now time to move on and leave John to face up to what he had done — for the first time in his life.

* * *

John Whitehouse was finding life on remand in one of Her Majesty's toughest prisons hard to adjust to. He wasn't the first MP to find himself behind bars, and he wondered how others had coped. He seemed to remember one high-profile politician writing a book about his experiences. Apparently he'd survived by becoming a combination of a teacher, an agony aunt and an amateur legal expert for the other inmates. Maybe John could do the same eventually but for now, he was just trying to survive a day at a time.

Today was better than most, though,

because he was expecting a visitor.

John was sitting at a table in the visiting room trying not to make eye contact with any of the other men. It was humiliating to be sitting there in grey sweat pants like everyone else, a bright orange bib over his grey sweatshirt.

Robert Cross, his political agent, shuffled over to the table and sat down. He couldn't have looked more unhappy to be there if he'd tried.

'Thanks for coming, Robert,' John said. 'It means a lot.'

'No problem,' Robert said without making eye contact. 'I've brought the clothes you asked for.'

Remand prisoners were allowed to wear their own clothes and Robert had been the only person John could think of to ask to bring them. His brother was refusing any contact with him and John had given up trying to get in touch for now.

'How are things on the outside?' John asked, his light tone trying to recreate the usual mood of the conversations between the two men.

Robert sighed. 'Look, John, I've come today to make a few things clear.'

He paused. John had been writing to him daily since he arrived at the prison. Pages-long letters with instructions for how to take things forward in the constituency and planning ahead to the next election. The man was deluded.

'John, it's time to face up to reality. You're going to be away for a long time. The wheels are already in motion to remove you as our MP. The party has already selected a shortlist for their next candidate . . . '

Robert stopped when he noticed the look on John's face. It was as if someone had switched off a light behind his eyes.

Robert felt terrible for being the one to cause that look of defeat. But then he remembered what his former employer had done.

Robert stood and held out his hand to John, who simply sat slumped in his chair.

Robert left the room and went to collect his phone and other belongings that had been confiscated on his way through the security checks. It was the first time he'd entered a prison and he hoped it would be the last. He certainly wouldn't be visiting John Whitehouse again.

Robert had always been a loyal and hardworking agent to the candidates in his constituency. When John Whitehouse had been elected, it had been the pinnacle of Robert's career and he'd thoroughly enjoyed the previous couple of years.

However his association with the disgraced MP would stain his reputation for the rest of his life and he would never forgive him. He had come here today to draw a line under their professional relationship and to make it clear that Whitehouse should stop contacting him. He'd achieved what he set out to do. So why did he feel so bad?

Robert pondered this all the way home and came to a conclusion that was fairly obvious.

The chain of events that John Whitehouse had started with his crazy scheme hadn't just affected those who were touched by it directly. Like ripples from a pebble thrown into a lake, the effects of Whitehouse's actions had spread out and touched many people's lives.

Robert supposed he was one of the lucky ones. At least he hadn't ended up dead.

17

It finally looked as though all the loose ends in the case were tied up. Dave had never been more grateful to close a file in his whole career. It had been one of the hardest periods of his life, both professionally and personally.

With all the court cases prepared and passed to the Crown Prosecution Service, he could at last relax on that score.

His dad was on the mend, so another of the stresses he'd been under was taking up less of his time and energy. Dad was going to move in with Anne for a while. Dave felt a small twinge of guilt because he saw this as killing two birds with one stone — Dad would be well looked after and his sister wouldn't have as much time on her hands to fuss around Dave. With his relationship with Morven in its early days, he could do without her meddling. He thought back to the awkward conversation he'd had with Anne the other day.

'I'm a big boy now,' he'd said gently. 'I really can take care of myself, you know.'

'Yes, but you know I enjoy looking after you,' Anne protested.

'Listen, I've met someone. We've started seeing each other and it just seems at bit, well, odd to have my sister doing all this stuff for me.'

At first Anne had looked a little upset but then a smile crept over her face.

'About time too,' she said at last. 'Maybe she'll be able to stop you spending all your time at work.'

Dave was relieved she'd taken it so well. He would have hated to hurt his sister's feelings and he really was grateful for all she'd done for him in the past. They would always be close and he felt lucky that she was happy for him.

'You'll have to bring your new lady friend round for a meal once Dad's settled in,' Anne said.

Dave grimaced. *One step at a time*,

he thought. He wanted to enjoy his new relationship for a while before he risked Morven meeting Dad and Anne — he knew it wouldn't be long before Morven was subjected to the family photo albums.

* * *

Since getting together with Dave, or perhaps more likely since her parents' killer had been behind bars, the distressing dreams that had plagued Morven for ten years had stopped. She occasionally still had dreams of her parents, but they now featured only pleasant memories instead of dark ones from the night of their murders.

Morven was glad she hadn't stopped dreaming about her mum and dad altogether. In a way, the dreams kept them alive and reminded her of all the happy holidays and family celebrations they'd enjoyed.

Eva Clarke had loved Christmas especially, and the house had always been decorated for the whole of December.

Every year Elly would come downstairs to a room full of gifts. James Clarke always tried to pretend he was more of a 'Bah Humbug' person but he always ended up joining in with whatever Eva had planned.

Most years Adam McLean and his wife had joined them for Christmas dinner, but in Morven's dreams it was always just the three Clarkes. Morven didn't know whether she would ever be able to think about Adam McLean without feeling a sharp pain in her heart.

Now, though, she was able to look forward to the future with optimism. Although it was early days in her relationship with Dave Bradley, things were going really well.

He was still a workaholic — Morven didn't think she'd ever be able to change that, even if she wanted to. Dave was brilliant at his job and because she had been part of his working life, Morven completely understood his commitment to it.

They had fallen into a habit where

Dave came round to Morven's apartment most evenings after he finished work. They'd even been on a couple of 'real dates', one to a restaurant and one to a work colleague's birthday party. It had felt odd walking in together but nobody had so much as raised an eyebrow.

'Everyone's been waiting for the two of you to get together for ages,' Elizabeth Foster told her with a smile when she mentioned it.

* * *

Morven thought she and Dave were going to spend the weekend at her apartment getting to know each other better. Now all the paperwork on the abduction case was taken care of, Dave was able to take two days off for the first time in months.

He was due to arrive early on the Saturday morning and Morven was looking forward to the weekend, if slightly nervous about what would happen when it came to Saturday night.

Up to now Dave had been returning

to his own home, or to the office, after they'd spent the evening together. Kisses and cuddles on the sofa were the closest they'd come to intimacy. And although she hadn't admitted it to anyone, Morven was still unable to sleep in her bedroom. Once Dave had left she would retrieve the quilt from her bed and make herself as comfortable as she could back on the sofa.

She'd told Dave about her idea of finding somewhere else to live, but he hadn't been keen on it.

'It's never a good idea to make major decisions so soon after a traumatic experience,' he said. 'Sorry, I'm sounding like a psychologist but I've seen it happen to friends. They usually end up regretting whatever the decision was.'

He was, however, enthusiastic about Morven's plans for sinking a sizeable amount of money into helping victims of violent crime. They hadn't discussed Morven's wealth yet but Morven loved the way he still treated her the same, regardless of her money. He was happy to pay when they'd been out to eat but he didn't make a big deal of it when Morven insisted she would pay next time.

When Dave arrived right on time, letting himself in with the security codes Morven had given him, Morven could tell he had a surprise for her by the grin on his face.

'I hope you're not going to mind,' he said. 'I know I should've asked you first but once I had the idea I couldn't stop myself booking it.'

'What?' Morven was half intrigued, half dreading hearing what Dave had booked.

He showed her his phone screen which was signed into the website of a beautiful country house hotel in Sussex.

'Just the one night,' he said. 'I'm not made of money, you know.'

Morven laughed when she realised he was winding her up.

'It looks great. Give me twenty minutes to pack.'

Morven hurried to her bedroom

while Dave went to the kitchen to make himself a coffee. On the way he passed the open door to Paula Gill's old room. It was the first time he'd seen inside and he was surprised.

'You've cleared everything out of your spare room,' he shouted through to Morven.

'Yeah. I didn't want anything left to remind me,' she called back to him.

Paula's dad had turned up a few days earlier to pick up the bags that Paula had left behind. He'd found it hard to meet Morven's eyes as he shifted all the stuff out of the apartment.

'We're sorry,' he said as he left. 'Me and her mother, we never brought her up to behave that way.'

Morven hadn't been able to bring herself to try and make him feel any better. The Gill family would have to come to terms with what Paula had done by themselves.

Dave and Morven set off in his car, heading for the Sussex countryside. It was a lovely spring day and they were both looking forward to a couple of days away from the city. Yet both of them were apprehensive about the night ahead.

Dave had worked out that it wouldn't be a good idea to try to take things further with Morven at the apartment. He'd noticed her unwillingness to go into her bedroom, other than to put clothes away or do other quick tasks like packing this morning. However he hadn't wanted to force the issue by trying to talk to her about it.

Not realising that Dave was aware of her inability to sleep in the room where she'd almost been killed, Morven had been starting to think Dave wasn't as attracted to her sexually as she was to him. Surely he would have made some sort of move by now if he was? She was failing miserably at trying not to overthink their relationship.

As they neared their destination, Dave started to worry about things from another angle. If Morven thought he was taking her away with the sole intention of sleeping with her, would that make her back off? It had taken him ages to decide whether to book one room or two. In the end he'd contacted the hotel and found out they had two adjoining rooms available.

The final decision on sleeping arrangements could be made later, but first there was the awkward business of checking in.

Morven hadn't even asked how many rooms he'd booked. If she'd been expecting to share, would she find his booking two rooms odd?

Dave could hardly recognise himself. He'd always been confident and self-assured when it came to his love life. Suddenly he was hesitant and nervous. Still, he'd never been involved with anyone who meant as much to him as Morven.

As it turned out, all his worry was for nothing.

'Oh, how lovely,' Morven said when they'd checked in and received their keys. 'I've never stayed anywhere that had adjoining bedrooms before. It's a gorgeous place, Dave. Thank you so much for bringing me. I think it's going to turn out to be just what I needed.'

The hotel had once been a rambling family home belonging to some earl or lord. Dave had read the history of it on the website but he couldn't recall many of the details. It had recently undergone a refurbishment, and the décor and furnishings were sumptuous. Dave had been attracted to it by the promise of peace and quiet and the spacious grounds where they could walk without worrying about traffic or bumping into too many other people.

As they reached the doors to their rooms, Morven gave Dave a quick hug and they arranged to meet up in half an hour.

'First one to unpack gets to unlock the door between the rooms,' Morven said, laughing.

* * *

Once they'd unpacked and changed, Morven agreed to Dave's suggestion of a stroll in the grounds of the hotel. They walked hand in hand in silence for a while, enjoying the peace and the fresh air.

Morven could hardly remember the last time she'd been out of London. She'd always lived in the city, and couldn't imagine living anywhere else, but in recent years she'd missed the trips to the country she'd enjoyed with her parents.

That reminded her of something she'd learned earlier that day.

'Oh, I forgot to tell you,' she said as they wandered beside an ornamental pond. 'I had an email from the witness protection people. They're going to officially close my case once Lee Robertson is sentenced.'

'Are you OK with that?' Dave asked. He knew she'd been getting used to the idea, but once it was made official, that would be it.

'Definitely. It makes total sense. It was only the killer being out there, knowing I could identify him, that made witness protection necessary in the first place. I can go back to having a normal life at last. Whatever that is.'

Dave hugged her, speaking into her hair as he tried to make her understand that he wanted to be a part of that normal life.

'It's all behind you now,' he said. 'It's time to stop looking back over the past ten years, thinking about what you've missed. Let me help you move on.'

Although it was spring, the day had started to cool so they returned to the hotel and ordered hot chocolate in the lounge. A couple at the other side of the room caught Morven's eye. They were sitting hand in hand and were deep in conversation. The thing that had attracted her attention was that they looked to be around the age her parents would have been now.

Would she ever get used to the stab of emotion that hit her every time she was reminded of the years her parents had missed?

Morven supposed it was only natural

after recent events that they were at the forefront of her mind.

It wasn't until the drinks arrived that Morven remembered the last time she'd drunk hot chocolate. Jenny Mason had drugged her by crushing sleeping tablets and mixing them into the hot, sweet drink. It looked as though her favourite drink would be off the menu for a while, until time blurred that memory.

'I'm sorry,' she whispered to Dave. 'I'm not going to be able to drink it after all.'

As soon as she explained why, Dave felt like an idiot for even suggesting it. By the time he'd arranged for a different drink for Morven, she was dozing in front of the crackling fire.

Dave sat and watched her for a while, thinking how lucky he was to be sitting here with her. Things could have turned out so differently. She'd survived being taken hostage, almost been killed by someone who was supposed to have protected her, and God knows what Lee Robertson had planned for her when he followed them to London.

Dave wished he could suspend this moment in time so they could stay here together forever. Then, being his usual practical self, he amended that wish. It wouldn't be good for them to be stuck in one place forever. Far better to simply wish they could spend the rest of their lives together.

Once Morven woke from her nap they decided to go and change for dinner. Dave had booked a table in the hotel's restaurant which was famous for the chef's extravagant creations.

The meal was a delight and after a quick drink in the bar they both agreed it was time to call it a night.

Later Dave would look back and wonder why he'd spent so long worrying about their first night together. When they arrived at Morven's door they enjoyed a lingering kiss in the hallway before realising that they might as well go inside — Dave could reach his room though the adjoining door, after all. But neither of them intended for him to do that.

'Stay with me tonight,' Morven said breathlessly.

'Are you sure?' Dave said. 'I don't want you to think I've just brought you here to . . . '

He was silenced by another passionate kiss.

* * *

Room service breakfast was as delicious as the previous evening's dinner had been. Dave was starting to wish he could have booked for more than one night but as always, he had responsibilities at work to return to on Monday. But that left the rest of today to enjoy with Morven.

'What shall we do today?' she asked as she finished the last of her coffee.

'Well, I do have one idea,' Dave said, a wicked smile on his face. 'Seems a shame to waste the other bedroom.'

He led Morven through the door into his room and they collapsed onto the perfectly made bed, both overcome with fits of laughter.

* * *

The weekend had confirmed for both Morven and Dave that they had finally found the person they had been looking for. However by Monday, they were both keen to throw themselves into new challenges.

Dave was engrossed in a new case while Morven was working on her plans for helping victims of violent crime. She would turn the spare room into an office and planned to work from there for now. She couldn't think of a better way to exorcise the ghost of that time in her life.

Since returning from Sussex she'd also been able to sleep in her bedroom again — though it helped that she now usually had company.

The only decision Morven still had outstanding, now that the complicated business of her witness protection had been sorted out, was what to call herself. She had been Morven Jennings for ten years now and it felt like that was who she should be. But Elly Clarke was the daughter of two parents she had loved deeply and who had loved her with all their hearts. Shouldn't she go back to being that person?

It was a dilemma she wrestled with for days. Eventually she asked Dave's opinion. He was the most important person in her life now and he'd convinced her how much she meant to him.

'I've only known you as Morven and it certainly suits you,' he said.

'But what about my surname? Jennings will always remind me of Jenny.' A shadow passed over Morven's face.

'You really don't need to worry too much about your surname, you know,' Dave said with a smile. 'I'm hoping that very soon you'll be changing it — to Bradley.'

They kissed — as passionately as it was possible to do when they were both beaming with joy.

Other titles in the
Linford Romance Library:

DUKE IN DANGER

Fenella J. Miller

Lady Helena Faulkner agrees to marry only if her indulgent parents can find a gentleman who fits her exacting requirements. Wild and unconventional, she has no desire for romance, but wants a friend who will let her live as she pleases. Lord Christopher Drake, known to Helena as Kit, her brother's best friend, needs a rich wife to support his mother and siblings. It could be the perfect arrangement. But when malign forces do their best to separate them, can Helena and Kit overcome the disasters and find true happiness?

MY SUNSHINE

Anne Holman

Having escaped a controlling relationship, won the lottery and given up work, Jenny is adrift at twenty-nine. Then her landlady's widowed son Alexander seeks her help in a family emergency, and she is catapulted into a different world of muddy boots, wayward pets and three children in need of love and a firm hand. But Jenny is conflicted — to fall for Alexander means absorbing so much responsibility, and then there's his obvious uneasiness when it comes to her fortune. More importantly, do Alexander's feelings match her growing love for him?